Praise for Livia Llewellyn's *Furnace*

"Livia Llewellyn arrived as ~ ⸍ ⸍ . *Furnace* proves it once again. L ⸍l horror puts her in the conversa when it comes to important litera

—⸍⸍⸍u Barron, author of *⸍⸍ ueautiful Thing That Awaits Us All*

"Livia Llewellyn is one of the finest writers of dark fiction working today. Her lush prose draws you into worlds both strangely familiar and shockingly surreal. The stories, a dark playground of despair, nightmares, and desire, set their hooks into you and refuse to let go, long after you've finished reading. *Furnace* is astounding."

—Damien Angelica Walters, author of *Sing Me Your Scars* and *Paper Tigers*

"Short horror fiction is in a golden age, and Livia Llewellyn's short stories help make it so; they're fearless, ferocious, and compelling."

—Ellen Datlow, editor of *The Best Horror of the Year*

"The pitch-perfect work of Livia Llewellyn is visionary and dangerous; it's both extreme and unforgettably lyrical. Every accolade you've heard about this mesmerizing master of horror and her work is true. *Furnace* is a literary event of the highest order!"

—Joseph S. Pulver, Sr., editor of *The Grimscribe's Puppets*

"Stark emotions and vivid sexuality coalesce in Livia Llewellyn's fiction. Her stories manage to be raw in their intensity yet elegant in their delivery, making Livia one of the most exciting writers to emerge in recent memory."

—Justin Steele, *The Arkham Digest*

FURNACE

Other books by Livia Llewellyn

Collections:

Engines of Desire: Tales of Love & Other Horrors

FURNACE

LIVIA LLEWELLYN

WORD HORDE
PETALUMA, CA

First Edition

ISBN: 978-1-939905-17-8

A Word Horde Book
www.wordhorde.com

TABLE OF CONTENTS

To Brenda and Maeve Llewellyn Ihssen,
and all the other girls of the world.

PANOPTICON

Is this you?

There is a place deep in the warehouse district, far outside the civilized edges of the city called Obsidia, where the population bleeds off into cul-de-sacs and dead-end roads, where only abandoned brick buildings and crumbling smokestacks remain. You have heard of this place solely by learning to phrase the questions as though they were snowflakes falling from the sky—questions outside your control, beyond your care or concern. Questions like that are answered in the passage of time, eventually: by cracked nails pressed against yellowing maps of long-dead subway lines, words parsed from veins of blood welling from a blossoming wound, grunts behind locked bathroom doors that echo out numbers, names. Answers, in the smoky plume of the dragon, the sour tang of the drug. And over the years and decades, you bead the collected answers onto the needle-fine wire of your need: gradually a map appears, a date, a time. You will not hold this information a second time: the invitation, like a comet, will pass from your view into the black of night, never to be seen in your lifetime again.

It never occurs to you not to go. In a way, you're already there. Is this you?

***

Wheels screech against tracks, and sparks bounce off the pitted concrete walls. The train shudders as it plunges underground, and your cotton skirt slides with you over the curve of the orange plastic seat. No one else is in the car, so you slip onto the raised bump between seats, letting the V of the ridge rest firm between your legs. It calms you. Spaces are meant to be filled.

Opposite, posters fill the space between the windows and doors. Women and men with once-glowing cheeks and plump lips hold bottles of effervescing liquids, or lounge on sleek leather Biedermeiers, gazing through curtainless windows into Obsidia's glorious silver horizon, into a future that will never be. Their faces are faded, melted and mottled from mold, humidity, and relentless plumes of metallic smoke. The engines shudder again, and fluorescent panels buzz and wink out, one by one. At each far end, windows glow, illuminating the cars before and behind. You stand up and walk forward, your hand gripping the filthy poles and bars to keep your balance. The door to the next carriage is locked: you peer through the grimy windows and across a small rattling platform into sulphur-tinged light, your breath fogging the glass.

They can't see you, the couple in the car. You stand in black, swaying in time with the pitch of the train, watching the woman's head jerk back and forth. A man stands before her, hands clasping the looped bars overhead. His pants hang below the curve of his naked ass, and he thrusts his pelvis forward and back, in time to the rocking of the car. You move to the window's side, and catch flashes of long, wet cock, thrusting to and fro in the woman's mouth and hands. The flesh between your legs swells and thickens in the heat, and your fingers twitch: but you turn away, walk back into the empty dark of the car, whispering a number, a name. The train seems to sigh in return, murmuring hot phrases of love. So easy, to lean against the trembling doors. The upturned handles, so very hard, so warm…

Not yet, you whisper in the dark to the racing machines, to your racing heart.

Not yet.

Is this you?

***

The afternoon is the caramel shade of fossilized saurian bone, hardened and inured to the passage of time. You walk down streets razed by wind and dust into thin crusts of cobblestone and tar, the destination always on the tip of your tongue like the taste of anthracite coal. Signs have long decayed into dust in this part of the city, and only ravens and dogs know the lay of the land. But the jewels of information gathered over the years are a crown, and for this single day you are Queen. And the kingdom waits. Left of the summit breaker, her broken windows winking like sequins on a dead bride's gown. Right of the seven brick stacks, blackened with centuries and cloaked in webs of dead vines. Across the iron bridge and over the Mannequin Sea, its million sloe-eyed beauties jumbled below like broken teeth against a giant's fist. Painted, flaking pupils stare up at you, a stagnant sea of watchers: you look away, and run. Through the endless warehouse rows, low grey bunkers like scabs on necrotized flesh, long emptied of goods and dreams. You squat once, by the side of the road, and watch the strand of urine slither into the street, seep into the cracks of the worn stones. In seconds, all traces of you disappear. For one fearful moment, you see yourself as though through distant glass: cunt pressed onto the smooth rock, cobblestones melting and pressing up through the wet folds, the stony cock of the world fucking and drilling into your soul. You rise, scurry away. The cracked stones beneath your feet shift and moan.

At the end of the warehouses, a single building stands, framed by two coke quenching towers. A blast furnace winds its way into the center of the brick, pipes as wide as buildings split into massive V's that cast shadows into the sunless sky. Beyond the building, Obsidia disappears, as if the earth itself ends. This is it. There is nothing beyond.

Cracked engines line the walkway leading up broken steps to a single open door, leading into a void. You check your watch. You know the time to enter. You sit on an engine, in the shadow of the furnace, and wait.

Is this you?

***

At the right hour, at the right minute, when the seconds have burned away like beads of sweat on a lover's shivering back, you rise and walk with stiff legs up the steps. The air is still and thick, with motes of dust hanging about you like drifting spiders. The light ends in a clean line as you pass through the door, into a hallway that pierces through the wide factory space. If anyone else is here, you cannot hear them, cannot smell them. The dirt beneath your feet lays undisturbed. Those who dwell here did not come this way. Behind you, the door closes, the day disappears. Somewhere in the building, machines spring into life, their rhythmic thunder reverberating through the walls.

Doors line the hall, but you do not touch the knobs as you pass by, though they look warm and inviting. None of those doors lead to what you were instructed to seek, what you asked to see. You walk carefully, one hand raised to brush stray webs from your face: as an afterthought, you look up. If there is a ceiling, it is not visible to your small human eyes. The walls rise straight up, as if into stars. You feel naked, as if something has peeled the edges of space away, inserting its gaze through dark matter and time all the way into the sticky center of your bones.

In the gloom, a pale sulphur glow of light flares into life: a beacon, beckoning. You approach, your fingers brushing over the mound beneath your skirt. The glass is curved at the edges, like the windows of the subway car, and rimmed by strips of hard rubber. Like aquarium glass: thick enough to keep the two worlds, the wet and the dry, from commingling. Palms flat against the glass, you lean forward, until the tip of your nose hits the surface, and your breath flows from your lips back into your mouth. Your body settles against the door—not a door, really, but an end, a terminus—and finds the ridged curves of a handle, smooth and warm, perfectly positioned by your accommodating, hidden hosts. Vibrations from the unseen machines whoosh throughout the building like blood through veins, into the quivering brass. The fabric of your skirt grows damp. The light in the other room intensifies. And now you see.

Is this you?

***

In the next room, a crowd of people clumps together in the confined tube of a shuddering subway car, their faces blank, like melting ice. A woman sits on the plastic bench, one leg hitched up and resting on the orange curves of the preformed seat to her side. Her dark hair floats like a mourning veil in wind, obscuring her face. On the floor before her, a man crouches, his tongue and lips moving over the red folds of her cunt, barely visible through the long, unruly V of black hair that envelops it. The metal and glass before you is as impenetrable as a blast door, yet you swear you can hear the sound of her breath bleeding into your ears, hear the subtle wet sounds of the man's tongue lapping, drawing the liquid out of her. The brass handle shudders and slips against your raw skin: your skirt is bunched around your waist, but you don't remember raising it. You push your groin forward, gasping as the woman thrusts against the man, straining her body against his large hands. Claw-like nails bite into her thighs, and where they strafe her skin, rubies ooze from the flesh, clattering onto the floor. The standing, swaying men and women ignore them: they have no ears, no eyes, no mouths. Only you see the man's hideous, lupine face, his darting tongue; only you smell the sea salt folds of the woman's flesh; only you hear the leviathan sounds well from her throat as she comes, the noise as deep and dark as the engines below. Only you asked to see.

The man rises, almost unfolding his bulky mass into the small space, pushing against the other commuters to make room. They clatter against each other, and you start in shock as a pale arm drops from a sleeve and floats to the ceiling. Another arm drops, followed by a head. One by one, the people crumble into brittle, bloodless pieces. Were they ever alive? Snowflakes of flesh and bone drift and knock about in the hot, noisy air. The car flooded and they are underwater, you realize, and the crowd nothing more than mannequins. But, then, how do the man and woman breathe?

The man brushes the bodies away like fire pushing through grass. He is all impassive muscles and phallus, every part of him forged. Diamonds and pearls ooze from the tip of his purple cock in liquid strands, spilling down the woman's breasts. She reaches up to brush them away, but the man grabs her thighs and lifts her torso high into the air, impaling her onto his cock as easily as if she were a summer cotton dress, to be bent and torn at will. Between your legs, the metal shifts and pierces upward, as if into your heart: the pain is so great, you cannot speak. Your nails claw at the glass, and small squeaks fill the burning air. Within the car, the woman slides onto the man, and sapphires bleed from her eyes; she opens her mouth, and more rubies stream out, emeralds and opals and stars. The man is a piercing sword, a burning blade, a broken train, and finally, finally, her head whips back and all that black hair floats away as she sees you, you see you and you see her and you both scream don't, stop, don't stop. Not yet.

You want to see it all.

Before you, the woman splits apart. Her limbs join the others, drifting in the ruby sea. They were not mannequins, after all. The man pushes her torso off his cock, thick pearls of semen dribbling in strands from the purple tip. They brush across your face, droplets catching in the curves of your mouth. The taste is flame and oil, and you feel your skin peel away. You never left the subway train. You never wandered an abandoned kingdom of wonders, you never entered a hall of a million doors. You never received answers to all the questions you asked. You do not watch. You were never the audience. You were the space, the void. In the distance, sighs and faint applause; and the unseen engine winds down, each thunderous pound like a bead falling off a strand, with more and more space in between. Until, there is no sound at all, not even the crackle of fire or drip of blood. There is only you as the metal thrusts up past the walls of your cunt and splits you apart, you looking up past the endless walls past the brief flash pleasure into all-consuming frenzy of pain, you floating through a ruby ocean of your own making into a space where all the stars look down on you, and all the stars are eyes.

And yet. And yet.

You still see.

Were you wrong? Is there more?

Is this really you?

***

Overhead, the slender pedestrian bridge stands fast against a saurian colored sky. Your painted, flaking pupils see it in slices, only through the rigid fingers of a hand—whose hand it is, you cannot tell. There are hands all around you, feet and torsos and heads, but you do not feel them as much as sense that they are there, jumbled about like autumn leaves. Like snow. You cannot feel any part of your body, or if it even remains a part of you. Maybe in some near acre or field, your hand obscures the view of other eyes, another face. Occasional storms smear black clouds overhead, and sometimes night falls, though it does not fall often in this forgotten district of Obsidia. Yet, the view never changes. Always and only, you see the bridge, the fingers, the bird-free sky.

Although, once in a very long while, you spy movement on the bridge, the hesitant gait of a traveler, a seeker crossing the iron trestles. They are heading toward a place they've only heard of in half-spoken words, coils of smoke and spatterings of blood. You see the traveler, fix your unmoving eye upon their familiar, yearning face, and the slender line of metal will become a hallway, a black vein that bleeds out into a trillion desires, then endless horror, then beyond. You want to cry out, *I know this woman, I know this journey, this place. Turn back. Don't go.* But your fading lips cannot part, and your torso is a hollow void. All you can do is watch with lidless eyes, watch each traveler arrive at the destination of their own making, and wait for the day when the sun runs down and the stars burn out in the sky, when there is nothing more to see, because there is nothing more. And then you will have what you asked for, so very long ago.

You will have seen it all.

This is you.

STABILIMENTUM

Thalia woke up with a small moan, a gasp of air escaping her mouth as her eyes opened to dim morning light. She stood before the open door of her bathroom, the small room as black and empty as an elevator shaft. Did she sleepwalk? No, that couldn't be it. She was only still so tired that she didn't remember getting out of bed. Just like the day before, and the day before—three months of this now, starting the day she moved in. Leaning against the door frame, Thalia flipped on the bathroom light, peering up at the ceiling as she waited for the vertigo to dissipate. Thirty floors above her, a small city pressing down. She felt it the most in this tight, windowless space, the gurgles of water and pinging of pipes, the crush of so many people above and around her, doing the exact same thing. She had wanted to live high above everyone, far away from the crowds. It never occurred to her that with so many tenants pressed together, she would never feel truly alone, never feel far away from anything at all. Everyone bleeding into each other's space—city living, get used to it. Thalia pushed the unease away, and reached for the toothpaste.

She only noticed it later, as she was getting ready to leave for work—looking up as she struggled with her hair, she spied a large brown spider trembling on invisible strands, high up in the far corner over her bathtub. Thalia stared, momentarily slack-jawed, as the creature seemingly floated through thick circles and curves of a white spiral pattern within the invisible rest of the web, its pace furious in tempo and intent. That was going to be one big damn web when it was finished. Which would be never.

"Do not have time for this," Thalia mumbled, half-tiptoeing, half-clomping through the living room in an attempt to keep the neighbors below from waking up and complaining yet again about high heels and noise. A single shake to the bright yellow canister from under the kitchen sink told her all she needed to know. Barely enough to kill it, but it was enough. She tip-clomped back into the bathroom, and rose the can high into the air. Another small gasp escaped her lips, and she leaned back against the door frame. Again, vertigo—always the sensation that she was rising, rushing upward into the clouds. She just needed more protein, that's all, maybe eggs for breakfast tomorrow instead of coffee and toast. Thalia aimed the can, and pressed her finger down. The first shot sent the spider spiraling down into the tub, and the second, weaker blast slowed its tremulous death throes just enough to assure her there would be no sudden revivals. Thalia felt the prickle of wet mist against her skin, and a second later, an ugly floral scent stung her throat and eyes. She backed quickly out of the bathroom, leaving the frail crumple of body and legs on the bathtub mat, a dot waving eight farewells. She'd deal with it when she got home tonight.

***

The apartment glowed from the ambient lights of two cities in two states—one of the reasons she decided to rent the space, even if it was well beyond her means. From the long living room window, thirty-seven stories below, the Hudson River caught the spark and flash of Manhattan and pushed it away with the night sky, as if to say—how could mere galaxies and stars be more beautiful than this? The views were even more jaw-dropping from higher up, or so she'd been told. Thalia tossed her coat and bag onto the couch, and drop-kicked her shoes into the corner by the front door. Corner. Spider. Charlotte and her web, with circles instead of words. Thalia sighed, suppressed a shudder, and walked through the bedroom, ignoring the familiar surge of upwardness effervescing through her veins as she stopped before the bathroom door. She hated this part most of all: take a small wad of carefully arranged toilet paper, clamp it down over the remains, then quickly lift it up and into the awaiting maelstrom of the toilet. The worst part was feeling the body crunch and pop beneath the tissue—no, worse would be mistaking it for dead, only to watch it dart from the paper onto her hand. It had happened before, too many times to recall. Thalia shuddered again, scratched the back of her hand, and turned on the light. Her gaze lifted to the corner, just to be sure—

"Fuck," she said, and jerked back against the door frame in shock. In the same corner, three fat spiders spun at a juggernaut pace. Not like the first, though—these were fatter, thicker, and no dancer's grace in their limbs. Charlotte's big sisters? Instead of a spiral pattern, they worked on series of concentric circles pierced with lightning bolt-shaped lines, a sticky bullseye hovering almost six inches from the wall. Thalia ran into the living room, hands brushing and slapping at her hair, her face, her shoulders, her hair, her arms, her hair—an instinctual dance from early childhood that she'd never forgotten. Shit, she forgot to pick up more bug spray. Thalia stopped in the city-lit living room, hugged herself tight as she stared back at the yellow rectangle of light that was her bathroom.

"No fair," she whispered to no one in particular. It had taken all of her savings and a loan from her 401(k) to move from her apartment in the roach-infested, hundred-year-old tenement building into this seventy-story dagger of glass and light. Pristine, clean, new. There shouldn't be insects here, so high above the earth. There shouldn't be anything unclean.

Hairspray was her only choice. She slithered back into the bathroom, only after slipping a hoodie out of her dresser and zipping it up tight, so her hair would stay protected. All the other corners in the bathroom, in the entire apartment, were clean—what was the attraction to that particular triangle of plaster and paint? Thalia grabbed the hairspray off the counter and let loose. One by one, the spiders' movements slowed, then stopped altogether as they froze under the tacky weight of the mist. Below, on the clear mat, the original Charlotte still lay, shriveled and alone. Thalia kept spraying until there was nothing left in the can. Screw the ozone layer. She had spiders to kill, and an apartment to protect.

Once they were still, Thalia slipped on her dishwashing gloves, covered her Swiffer in paper towels, then dragged it across the top of the ceiling, moving the mop's flat surface back and forth until every last spider and strand of web was caught. She didn't want to touch the towels, so she simply unscrewed the head of the mop and let it drop into the tall silver garbage can. What a waste of money. Then: original Charlotte. A wad of toilet paper and a single flush took care of the body, although she had to wet a second wad of paper to dab up a stray leg. The air reeked of lacquer and white jasmine blossoms. She'd never buy that brand again.

After Thalia took the trash down the hall to the chute, she sat on her bed, halfway between the bathroom and living room doors. Just sat there, staring at the corner over the bathroom. The walls and ceiling were creamy white, smooth, placid as water, placid as the silence, punctuated only by a slight tick and groan of the plumbing behind the walls. What did the Charlottes know about that corner that she couldn't see? In her old apartment, it had been roaches in the kitchen and ants in the bedroom—typical problems for a typical big city apartment. Once she even found a squirrel gnawing its way through the window screen. But nothing as annoying—no, as creepy as this. Thalia shivered and held herself again. Outside, traffic and machinery hummed and throbbed its mechanical song to the autumn evening as if singing it down from the sky. Somewhere, wind whistled through an unsealed crack. The sound made her feel a million miles from nowhere. Thalia rose, and shoved some clothes in her gym bag. She just couldn't bring herself to use the shower tonight. Tomorrow, maybe, after she'd calmed down.

**

Two hours later, when she returned from the gym and a quick stop at the drug store, Thalia sprayed every corner in the bathroom and all along the floors, flat dread pressing against her lungs with every new reveal of wall from behind the furniture. But everything was clear. No spiders. The Charlottes were gone. Something unknotted from within her chest, and she let herself relax. Thalia ate a Stouffer's dinner, then watched TV for a while, her fingers tight around the delicate stem of a wine glass, three times full to the brim. She went to the bathroom, but only when she could hold it no longer—the entire time, she kept her eyes on the ceiling, her hand reaching blindly for the toilet paper. The vertigo hit her hard, and even in the bedroom now she felt its tug, like she was being sucked up into a drain. Thalia brushed her teeth at the kitchen sink, and washed her face there as well. Later, she slipped under the covers, but propped the pillows up, and left all the lights on, the hood of her sweatshirt firmly over her hair. She slept that way, book in one hand, cotton sheets clenched in the other, the small radio on her dresser crackling out words as if some sonic shield. What dreams she had, she couldn't remember. When the alarm woke her promptly at six in the morning, she once again stood in the doorway, eyes blinking in confused fear, fingers painfully splayed out into the dark as if holding everything above and behind the flimsy bathroom walls at bay. Thalia reached for the light switch, then looked up.

Over the bathtub, a black mass writhed around a giant, white-webbed X.

**

Her next-door neighbors, a couple who had heard her screams first, said they would let her call the super from their apartment, but only after she let them enter hers to see what was wrong, probably to make sure she wasn't exaggerating. One of the men made it as far as the bathroom door, then turned around, pale and silent. He rushed back into his apartment, and she heard him shouting into his cell phone only seconds later. The older man crept to the edge of the bedroom, and Thalia stood behind him, shivering and twitching, her fingers clenched around his arms. "Holy shit," he repeated, over and over. "Jesus Christ." One profanity for every ten Charlottes that swayed back and forth in the mass of webbing that took up the entire corner, and now filled the last third of the bathtub and draped over the shower curtain rod. Small, large, fat, thin, black, mottled grey; and all of them trying to make their way up to the ceiling, all of them spinning, spinning, spinning— Thalia's body gave a violent jerk, and she bolted from the apartment, unable to control her legs. Ten minutes later she found herself in the lobby, screaming incoherently at the doorman and lobby guards, at the police who had been called by the tenants who had heard her screams, by the super and the building manager. She opened her mouth and words rushed out, but they were no more comprehensible than the webbing upstairs, thick and grey and without any meaning she could understand. They spun, and she screamed, and outside the building, the city opened itself up into the day.

***

"Spiders love us," her mother always used to say, when Thalia was young. "They want to protect us from all the bad things—that's why they spin such large webs. The webs are a warning, that's all, to keep you from going near those bad things. Don't touch them, and they'll leave you alone." A child's fairy tale, a flimsy bandage for so much unexplained trauma. They'd crawl into her bed during hot summer nights, leave nickel-round bites of pale pink and blush-red on her shoulders and stomach that she discovered in the morning. She'd sit under trees reading books, look down, and find an army at her feet, making its way up her legs. Mosquitoes loved her sister, but they left Thalia alone. Thalia was reserved for the Charlottes of the world, for secret messages and images in the dots she could connect on her flesh, the maps and signs left in glistening strands against her pale bedroom walls. Whatever they were trying to tell her, it was swept away in the waterfalls of her fear, in the arc of a broom. Spiders were monsters, she came to believe. They didn't belong in this world of flesh and fur. They were terrible, and wrong.

Thalia dropped the copy of her lease onto the coffee table, hands trembling. She sat in the lobby, on one of the slick gray Italian leather couches artfully arranged before a two-story high waterfall bleeding off into a pool of fat, orange Koi. Late afternoon sun slanted through the light blue windows, turning the brushed steel walls into undulating sheets of mercury. She'd dreamt her whole life of living in a place like this, an antiseptic sliver of the future captured in the shape of a building and inserted into the grit and grime of the ordinary world. Didn't everyone want this? Now she was pinned here, like a butterfly to the board.

"I'm sorry," the on-site manager said. He sat opposite her, next to a woman with a sheaf of legal-looking documents in her hands, her fingers crawling over them like flesh-colored centipedes. A lawyer, sent from the corporation that owned the building. Occasionally the woman stared at Thalia and wrinkled her nose, as if she'd just caught a whiff of warm shit. The young man from the apartment sat on a chair, his visibly upset partner perched on the arm rest beside him. "You're three months into a five-year lease, whose terms you are aware of and approved when you signed. I know how upsetting this is, but breaking your lease because of a few spiders—"

"—few spiders," Thalia whispered, laughing. The sound caught in her raw throat, and she choked. "A few spiders."

"A small nest. A small infestation."

"There were hundreds," Thalia said. "Thousands."

"Oh, I doubt that—" he started to reply.

"No, she's right, we saw them too," the older man said. "Hundreds, at least."

"And they were all different kinds," Thalia continued. "How could they be from the same nest? And where did they all come from?"

The manager ignored her. "We had two professional exterminators examine your apartment. They found a small number of spiders, nothing unusual. It's autumn, they're moving indoors now. The exterminators thoroughly sprayed the bathroom, as well as the rest of the apartment and the hallways, and building services has already completely cleaned your bathroom and bedroom. All at no cost to you, of course. You should be able to return to your apartment tomorrow morning."

"What about the rest of the apartments on our floor?" the older man demanded. Daulton was his name, and his partner was Henry—that much Thalia had found out about them. Daulton held Henry's hand in a tight, nervous clench. "What about our apartment? Who knows what's hiding in the walls and ceilings and floors?"

The manager nodded his head, raising his hand in a faux-diplomatic gesture. Shush, it meant. Shut up. "We'll be spraying each apartment on the thirty-seventh floor, as well as the floors above and below. But this is not an extraordinary circumstance. Insects are not the fault of management, nor are they an act of God. You can break your lease if you wish—we certainly won't stop you. But you know the financial and legal penalties for doing so. Ask yourself if it's really worth the cost." He rose to his feet, and the woman followed suit, ruffling the papers before her like feelers. "Let me know what you decide. It's a beautiful building, and you've all been excellent tenants. We certainly hope you'll stay."

Thalia watched him melt away into the mercury of the lobby's shadows and corners. She stared at the copy of her lease, white paper leaves resting on burled and polished wood, her signature and initials scrawled across the pages, over and over again. "I can't go back," she said. "I can't go back."

Daulton reached out, touched her knee. "You can stay with us— sleep on the couch for a couple of days. Until you—until we all decide what to do."

Henry rose, clutching his copy of the lease. "Come upstairs. We'll order take-out and watch TV. No bug movies, I promise."

"Thanks." Thalia managed a wan smile at his joke. "I'll be up in a bit. I need some fresh air." She left her copy of the lease on the burl wood table.

The air was chilly and crisp, with a touch of moisture blown in from the waterfront. Thalia sat on the bench just outside the lobby doors, watching traffic rush back and forth before her, watching people walk and race home from the workday, clutching expensive satchels and bags. Leather footfalls, stilettos clacking, and the murmur of cell phones and car engines poured down the streets and over a horizon that looked no different than here. More buildings, cold and clean and tall. She looked up, bending her head back until she thought she'd fall over. The apartment building rose in a column of silvery blue glass, straight as a shark's tooth, until it pierced the fine clouds above and disappeared. Where it ended, she had never been able to see. Just above the white sky, she supposed. Or, did it simply go on and on, thousands of floors and tenants in dimensions she'd never live long enough and climb high enough to see? A wave of nausea slithered through her, and she bent her head over into her open hands, closing her eyes. All that weight hanging over her head, all those rooms, all those lives. Someday, something would have to give.

When it grew just dark enough that she could no longer see the end of the neon-lit street, Thalia forced her stiff limbs indoors and upstairs. Something would give, but it wouldn't be her, not today.

Every rising digital number in the elevator pushed a weight into her chest, floor by rising floor, and she felt time stretch and thin out as she moved further away from the earth's warm curve and closer to the clouds. Thirty-seven floors felt like thirty-seven thousand, and she felt her vertigo well up then drop away like the horizon's curve. When the elevator doors finally opened, she sniffed the carpeted hallway—a faint tang of chemicals, or perhaps her imagination, spurred by that familiar touch of vertigo, now more like a hand over her face. She walked past her door, quickening her steps as she reached Daulton's and Henry's apartment. When Henry opened the door, and the warm candle light and scents of dinner washed over her, she almost cried with relief. This was normal. This was safe. For now, this was home.

***

Thin mist distorted the distant lights of Manhattan into pixilated strands of winking dust. Below the waterfront's edge, the river flowed silent and ghost-black—a mirror no longer, but a void. Thalia sat on the edge of Daulton's and Henry's couch, staring at the two slumbering cities, so far below that they looked like constellations. It wasn't quite six, but already a touch of morning stained the edges of the sky, with a color she couldn't quite find the name for in her sleepy mind. Thalia rubbed her eyes, and let her head sink back against the couch, but only for a moment. It was time. She had to go back—she'd worn the same gym clothes for almost two days now, didn't have her purse or cell phone or wallet. And somewhere in a plastic file box next to the living room bookcase was the business card of the real estate agent who she'd paid to look over her lease four months ago. Maybe he'd see something, some loophole, some tiny flaw in the wording she could slip through to escape. Thalia bit her lower lip hard, hoping the pain would blot out sudden images of that dark mass of limbs, fat round bodies bobbing and darting in and out of each other, and the soft crackle of webbing sagging under all that weight—

Thalia rose and quickly walked to the front door, before she changed her mind. The hallway beyond was silent, bright with tastefully recessed fluorescent lighting. She stepped quietly onto the carpet as she closed the door behind her, and then stood frozen, her breath the only sound in the long corridor. Beads of sweat welled up from her skin, trickled down the sides of her cheeks, under her arms and breasts.

"Move," she whispered. Her body didn't respond. The word dropped into the silence and disappeared without a trace.

She looked down the hall, then turned. Identical doors in identical frames in identical walls, and behind them identical people sleeping, washing, eating, dressing. All of them, acting as if it were nothing to go through the motions of living a tenth of a mile or more above the surface of the planet, a tenth of a mile above everything else alive. Did any of them understand this miracle of engineering that was their modern life? Every one of them, herself included, floating, unmoored.

It almost felt like trespassing. Thalia made her way silently to her door, holding her breath for a long second as she stopped before it, staring at the dark brass plate bolted to the wood. The tiny dash between the floor and the apartment numbers had disappeared, leaving a monolithic-looking 3707 in its wake. She slid her key into the lock. The tumblers sounded like gun shots—Thalia glanced down both ends of the long hallway, expecting residents to pour out of their doors. Nothing happened. She pushed the door open a crack, sniffed the air. No odd smells. Thalia opened the door all the way, her eyes adjusting to the dim space. The living room and little galley kitchen seemed no different than usual. Thalia wondered if the manager might have been lying about calling exterminators and the cleaning crew. There was no way to know.

She reached out and pushed on the light switch. The outside faded to black as the room glowed. Thalia shut the door behind her, looking up to the ceiling, brushing her hand over her hair.

Except for the pictures she'd hung, the walls were bare; the corners, clean. She forced herself to turn left, walk to the bedroom door, and open it.

Across the inky darkness, the bathroom glowed. From the top of the door frame to the floor, every single inch of the opening was covered in thick white webbing, picking up the light from behind and reflecting it into the room like ripples of a wind-ruffled pond. In its middle, a single colossal X sat as unmoving and hard as a metal breaker on Normandy sand.

"Don't touch them, and they'll leave you alone," she blurted out, stepping back. Her sneakers grew hot and squishy with urine.

Behind the X, something large and shapeless moved. Thalia caught the curve of limbs. A saucer eye appeared, staring out at her through the gaps in the webbing, unblinking and curious. Behind the shape, no wall, no cabinet, no plastic shower curtain. Nothing remained that looked human-made at all.

Thalia grabbed the bedroom door with both shaking hands, closing it as quickly and quietly as possible. She ran to the couch, dumping her purse on the cushions, scattering the contents with her trembling fingers. The cell phone slid to the rug in a muffled thump. She scooped it up and stabbed at the keyboard. It took forever. Behind the ragged gasp of each breath, she waited for the inevitable scratch of something breaking free.

"Hello?" A man's voice—the building's super.

"Back, they're back, the spiders are back." Her jaws felt so tight, she could barely spit out the words.

"Lots of them?"

"A web over my bathroom door, covering the whole thing. Something's behind it—it's fucking *huge*. Bigger than me."

"Okay, hold on. I'm gonna transfer you to the other super." A steady mechanical tick washed into the line before she could protest. Thalia stared at the bedroom door, straining to hear any kind of movement or sound. Nothing.

"Yes," someone finally answered, in a thin and static-scratched buzz of a voice from a trillion miles away. "Hello?"

"This is three-seven-oh-seven," Thalia finally spoke. "I'm—"

"Three hundred seventy, apartment seven, right?"

"What? No, the thirty-seventh floor."

"My switchboard says you're calling from the three hundred and seventieth floor. Where are you now?"

Thalia squeezed her eyes shut. "I'm supposed to be on thirty-seven."

Silence. Then: "Ah. Are you alone?"

"Where the bathroom used to be. Behind the webbing—something large."

"The tenant. From apartment three hundred and seventy."

"Oh." Thalia dug her fingernails into her thigh, clenching until pain broke through the fear in clarifying waves. "So. We've both come—undone."

"Hold on." Another moment of silence, then: "I've put a call in to my team. The situation will be resolved. We've handled this problem before."

Thalia opened her mouth, tears streaming down her face. Her words broke apart into soft sobs. "Am I safe? What do you want me to do?"

"Sit tight, don't touch any webbing you see, and we'll get you back down."

"Okay."

The voice softened. "You'll be fine. Look out the windows, if you can."

"Why? What's out the windows?"

Faint strands of laughter floated across the line, scratchy and thin. "I don't know. I've never been down that far. But you should look—so I've been told."

"Why?"

"Because whatever's outside, you may never see it again."

Thalia inched toward the living room window, and pulled on the curtain cord. Bands of bright light washed over her, and she squinted, waiting for her eyes to adjust. Gradually, beyond the cold glass, the thinning mists, out of the starry morning air they appeared...

Her mouth opened. Nothing came out. Against her ear, the voice hummed and buzzed, fading to silence as the phone slipped from her hand to the floor.

***

Wind whistled through a hidden crack in the apartment, a melancholy siren song from beyond. Thalia sat on her bed, nursing large glass of wine. She had stood at the living room window for hours, hands and forehead pressed against the glass, legs cramped and trembling, eyes unblinking until tears ran down her face. Even then she didn't move, not until all those vast configurations, all the creatures that crept and floated and flew, finally began to slide up and out of view, until disappearing altogether in a wash of rain-heavy grey. And then vertigo had taken over once more, every fiber in her body shifting in the elevator creep of her slow descending floor.

Thalia emptied her wine glass, then slithered off the comforter and walked to the window. She had never been sure what or where she had been looking out at, in those few incredible hours, but it had been more vast and shining and wondrous than a thousand Manhattans under the glow of a thousand rising suns. Now, before her: sickly lemon squares of light glowing in the heavy rain of an early evening along the Hudson River. Behind her, under pristine ceilings and hundred-watt lights: familiarity, empty and small. And the apartment that she deserved, that she had always been meant to have: some three hundred stories beyond her reach.

Thalia pressed a hand flat and firm against her chest, fingers splayed wide and pressing into the bones. Fingers, delicate lines of flesh, holding everything back that wanted to burst forth. She stood in the gloomy dark before the window, mouth pursed, concentrating on the ebb and flow of the city she'd never escape, of the erratic beat of her trapped heart. Only when it slowed back into dull, predictable rhythm, a beat so feeble she couldn't feel it at all, did she take her hand away.

WASP & SNAKE

Wasp is given two choices by her client, each procured by the night market merchant. From where he bought these items, he will not, or cannot, say. The biomechanical finger sleeves are beautiful: bright copper filigree, each tip sharpened to points invisible, the better with which to dispense luminous poison hiding in the hollows, poison which will be secreted from her alchemically transformed flesh. Wasp raises her thin black hands to the candle light, admiring how the metal elongates her fingers into gleaming claws. With great reluctance, she slips them off. Beautiful, but finger sleeves will be seen—and, once welded to her flesh, never to be removed. Her life will revolve around her hands, around this irreversible decision. Hasn't life revolved enough already around things outside her own desires, the desires of others and the price they pay her to fulfill them? The merchant lifts up the other choice from its bed of wet velvet. It takes both hands, and Wasp's client, who is paying, has to help. They stand before her, the two men and their terrible cargo. Wasp lets out a slow breath, then nods. If all goes well, her life will forever change, for the better. Then someday, with another commission, she'll return for the sleeves—if only to use them to rip her own life from her throat.

***

25

Her screams cram up all unused cracks of the night. Many hear them. No one cares. The stone labyrinth of the underground market is constantly filled with such sounds, with human shrieks and screeches floating above the constant grinding, pounding, stitching of obscene machines. Bent forward over a rough wood table, the naked Wasp shudders. Her face presses down against a shallow groove, where so many others have worn the grain fine and smooth. If she looks up, her watering eyes sees fine sprays of her blood mist through the air, speckling walls already blackened with the blood of others who came before. Behind her, the merchant presses the electric hammer against her lower spine, and pulls the trigger again. Wasp dreams of slamming through the ground, her bones melding with saurian predators trapped miles below the surface of dead dried seas. Somewhere in the real world, the merchant bolts the second choice to her flesh, using living metals that flicker as they vibrate between one dimension and the next. The pain lightning-strikes its way up her torso, and the roots of the metal object follow like rivers of mercury, burrowing into her brain. He is welding her to a darker universe. When he is finished, he says, her body will be a pipeline to hell.

He's not opening a gate, Wasp thinks as she grimaces and howls. He's just widening the road.

***

Five weeks later, Wasp walks painlessly past colossal doors into the cathedral hall of the bank where she first met her client, a distant season ago. In her gloved hand is the badge that allowed her to spend the past four days here, filling ledgers with rows of neat numbers, stuffing memos into pneumatic tubes and shooting them deep into the ground. Today is the day. She stops with her back to the doors, staring over her shoulder in the high noon light at the blurred reflection behind her. Under the sweep of a slim linen jacket and a pleated silk dress, the biomechanical tail erupts from her spine and coils round her waist, a heavy belt waiting for a single thought, sharp clicks filling the air as chromium vertebrae unfurl to reveal the flickering shadow of a stinger, sharper than anger, longer than pain. Or so she imagines. You will never see the stinger, the merchant had said. It resides in another universe, only revealing itself fully when you insert it in the target—and then, of course, you will not see it at all. Of course, Wasp had replied, as she poured coins onto his table. They clattered in the shallows where her body had laid, the gold so pretty against the warm brown stains. Her client had come to her with that money, and the promise of much more if she succeeded, if she gave his unfaithful snake of a lover precisely what she deserved. You know what that means, he said. Wasp stared into smoke-stained skies as she gave her emotionless reply.

Only a killing blow will do.

***

The sun shifts, slips down iron and glass walls, and the hum of customers and office machines fills the space in an endless ambient drone. Wasp sees her target, a mid-level manager she only knows as Snake, near the end of the day. Snake is light-skinned, with short bobbed hair of glossy brown. She is pregnant—the product of her infidelity. She walks hand in hand with her husband as they make their way across the glossy marble to the edge of the office pen. The husband gives his wife a chaste kiss, and winds his way back across the floor, his shadow growing until it momentarily covers the room. Wasp rubs her ink-stained fingertips on a small cloth, and crouches over the ledger. She doesn't need to look. Snake steps behind the gated counter into the pen, heading to the opposite side of the floor. On her desk are neat stacks of paper that have accumulated during her absence, a two-week vacation spent with the man who approached Wasp last spring.

The day winds down. Wasp writes, and waits.

Bells chime overhead, announcing closing time. Wasp takes her purse and casually makes her way through the pen to a wood door marked EMPLOYEES. Just like the last four days, she walks down the hall to the women's powder room, where she refreshes her face and makes small talk with the other clerks. The room empties out while she lingers in the stall, then Wasp slips into the small utility closet. In the dark space, Wasp sits, the tail warm at her waist, the stinger vibrating in a pocket of some unseen cosmos between her legs as she runs over the plans in her mind again, again, again, each end to her assignment the gruesome same.

Pity about the child.

***

Naked, Wasp stands at the edge of the pen, holding her breath. Before her, the empty bank floor stretches into quiet dark like an abandoned church—at the far end, a single green-shaded banker's lamp glows. She moves like liquid, letting the tail unfurl and sway, navigate her body through the shadows with barely any effort of her own. Snake raises her head only at the last minute, when Wasp lets out a small sound, just enough to make her swivel the chair around. Wasp stares at Snake's face, her widening eyes. She feels the tail rise up, the stinger shiver: does the woman see it? And Wasp's tail plunges the stinger into the woman's chest. In the silent hall, there are no screams, only the crash of wood to the floor, the hard breathing of the two women, the soft gush of blood. They lie together like lovers, Wasp mounted on the woman with the chromium prosthesis burrowing deep into red.

Snake's lips move.

Wasp leans in.

Snake speaks again, words Wasp barely hears above the laughter.

My husband thanks you.

And the road widens, and Wasp feels the stinger open, and her mind grows small. She would draw back, pull out, but her flesh is nothing now, her body is not her own, there is only the tail and the stinger, sucking whatever gestates inside Snake into Wasp's swelling flesh. There won't be enough room. Even with the two of them, conjoined by the expanding tail, there won't be enough room for whatever is about to be born.

A pipeline to hell, the night market merchant had said. He never did tell her which way the darkness would flow.

CINEREOUS

Paris
October, 1799

The nails on the heels of Olympe Léon's boots are the only sounds in the silence of night's chilly end. Click click click through indigo air, like the metallic beat of a metronome's righteous heart. As always, when she sees her destination at the end of rue St. Martin, rising black and monolithic against the encroaching country and graying sky, her heart and feet skip beats. She thinks of each single drop of blood, spurting and squirting from the bright flat mouths of the necks, and her small calloused hands and wide bowls to catch them all. Olympe, like all the assistants, is very proud of her training, and very afraid of losing her place, very afraid of sinking back into the city's bowels, never to return. She never misses a drop.

The building has no name. It never has. Inside the courtyard, men in effluvia-stained coats scurry back and forth to one of the three large guillotines sitting on the worn packed earth. Scientists and doctors and handlers, each carrying out their part of the Forbidden Experiment. Olympe and the young assistants are forbidden to venture beyond the warren of labs and rooms on the ground floor. The rules of their mysterious, tight-knit society haven't stopped her, but after two years, she has still only seen glimpses of the eight labyrinthine stories that loom in a perfect square around the courtyard, occasionally flashes of people moving up and down the wide staircases, and the constant winking of the stairwell candle flames high above her like trapped stars in the artificial night. Most floors are reserved for research. The top two floors, merged long ago into a single high-walled prison, is where the Forbidden Experiment has taken place for over twenty years now, and only handlers are allowed inside. Thick-limbed men swathed in heavy layers of leather and chain mail, with animal-faced masks and gloves of unyielding steel, unlock the doors to the top floor once every week, and venture into a metal bar-ceilinged warren of broken rooms and passages, untamed flora and small creeping fauna, a facsimile and perversion of the natural world, open to the elements yet contained and confined. And after a time, each handler emerges with a young boy or girl who howls and shits and pisses and bites like a wolf, a child who has had no interaction with the civilized world since birth. *Les enfants sauvages*. Some are sent to labs on the middle floors for dissection and vivisection and resurrection, some are taken to the basement levels for electrical and mechanical experiments beyond even Olympe's delicious imagination. And those tagged for the living head experiments are sent to the courtyard, to the guillotines and to her.

Olympe hangs her coat up in one holding room, and slips on her laboratory overcoat in another. She cannot describe how proud she feels when she buttons up the faded, fraying fabric. Out there in the world there are women who read books, who study, who are scientists and doctors as much as they can be, considering women are nothing more than failed men, walking fœtuses who never developed into their full male potential. Olympe, the brothel-raised daughter of a long-dead revolutionary and a long-dead whore, is very aware she will never be one of those women, those forward-thinking academic lights of France's glorious new future, but at least she is more than what awaits her outside the double steel courtyard gates, and it never fails to thrill her. True, the great men who conduct these incredible experiments tend to recruit uneducated yet comely young women and men like herself, who don't protest when a suck or two is requested of them, but Olympe is pretty and clean and always willing to comply. And she's smart. As she grabs her copper bowls and heads into the courtyard, she thinks of the top floor, that mysterious jungle of rooms and wilderness, of the cleverly concealed panopticons inserted throughout the rotting passages and hallways from which the scientists can fully observe the enfants sauvages without interaction or detection. Thanks to her strong fingers and nimble tongue, she's been in those rooms. She's seen what goes on in the artificial wild, she's heard what the scientists say. None of the other assistants have. None of them have ambitions quite like Olympe.

Each slender wood guillotine has a name, and something of its own personality, or so Olympe would like to believe. She's worked at the bases of La Bécane and Le Massicot, both nimble and effective apparatuses, but her heart and hand belong to the swift and silent blade that descends through the center of Mirabelle. There's just something about the sharp low whomp of Mirabelle's heavy mouton and blade rushing through meat and bone that satisfies Olympe in a way nothing else does. Already Le Massicot has been at work—Nana is at the neck of a sauvage, her copper bowl catching the blood which will later be sent rushing through tubes and vials in some candlelit room upstairs. Étienne stands slightly behind her, one large hand on each side of the head as he holds it still and upright for display. Blood trickles and pools around his shoes. Before him three doctors crouch, touching the head lightly with calipers and other devices, taking notes as they speak in low tones. They are measuring the lingering signs of a life taken so swiftly by the blade that the head often fails to acknowledge the body's demise. Olympe has seen the eyes of severed heads blink, seen lips twitch and heard gasps and sighs. The doctors hold vials up to the mouth to catch escaping vapors, peer through pieces of glass into the gaping neck, slide lances and needles into the jelly eyes.

The assistants know better than to ask what knowledge they seek, or what use they intend with it. Later, the living heads, as they are called, will be placed in large glass containers filled with viscous liquids, and join other similar containers on the fourth floor. Olympe has seen that secret, many-shelved room as well, seen the hundreds of surprised faces peering out from their amber-colored shells. She knows a good scientist must have a strong stomach and heart, but she has no real desire to return any time soon.

Mirabelle's wood frame is dull brown, the same color as Olympe's carefully pinned and bonneted hair. Lorilleaux is at his usual spot beside her, pulling worn leather gloves onto his long hands. When he clamps his fingers around the sides of each head nestling in Mirabelle's curved embrace, it's like watching a monstrous spider clamp down on its prey. An executioner stands on Mirabelle's opposite side, checking the ropes and mechanisms, giving one last polish to the blade. Sometimes the sun makes its way into the courtyard, bouncing between the windows and shining steel until it hurts to see. This morning the sky is cloudy and dull, and a fine haze floats through the air, a mixture of smoke and ash from the building crematorium and furnace fires that are never extinguished. The smell is particularly hideous today—for several weeks, an illness has steadily made its way through the sauvages, a flesh-destroying disease the doctors have yet to discover the cause of or cure for, a bodily putrefaction that gives an extra tang to the feathery airborne remnants of the dead. It coats the back of their throats and settles in their chests—everyone who works outside coughs, swallows constantly, drinks water and spits out discolored globs of phlegm. Olympe stares at the blanket of clouds rolling across the squared acre of sky over her head. It looks like another courtyard, a cold and lifeless mirror of the one below. She lays her copper bowls out on the long table positioned next to the stone platform on which Mirabelle stands. There is always a small space reserved for her, at the end of all the instruments and equipment the physicians and scientists use. Today is busy—there will be three subjects from the top floor coming to each guillotine. And when Olympe isn't collecting the blood and handing it over to whoever has reserved it, she will be expected to hand instruments to those who need them, refill pens, provide fresh paper, and occasionally bring out trays of coffee and sweets. In her coat pocket, though, is her own small notebook and pencil. When time allows, she scribbles down her own set of notes, just as any good scientist would, even though she isn't quite sure how to correctly shape all the letters or spell all the words.

Lorilleaux lets out a quick gasp, and Olympe turns. Something is wrong, she realizes, and her heart skips another beat. Across the courtyard, Mirabelle's first visitor of the day approaches. A handler has one of the diseased sauvages locked in an iron jacket attached to a long pole at the back, which he uses to push the body forward—a device the handlers created when the creatures are ill, when they don't want contact with the body. The sauvage lunges and stumbles on twig-thin legs, reaches out with broken-fingered arms, as all the creatures do. But, giant strands of spittle hang from its cracked black lips, and its pallor is that of a month-old corpse, as if every particle of health had been siphoned away. And its movements are slow, Olympe notes; sluggish and confused as if fighting off a fever or waking from the too-long grip of a terrible dream. One low continual moan issues from deep within its ribcage, not the high healthy roar she's used to hearing. Around the handler and creature, physicians and scientists scurry, already throwing out theories and furiously writing down notes. One of those physicians is Marie François Xavier Bichet, favorite student to the now-deceased founder of their society, Pierre-Joseph Desault—whose own head, it is whispered, now sits blinking and gaping in some forgotten corner of the building. Bichet never appears in the courtyard unless occasion merits, unless some important discovery is about to be made.

Olympe steps to the end of the table and grabs a bowl, hugging it to her chest like a shield as the phalanx of chaos approaches. The blade rises to the top of Mirabelle, and the executioner locks the déclic and release handle into place. Lorilleaux is several meters away, on the opposite side of the table. Olympe likes his gentle disposition, but she's never seen anyone who can make a living lifting heads from dead bodies yet tremble like a girl at the sight of anything worse than a bruise. He'll never be a doctor. The handler has unlatched the pole from the metal chest plate, and another handler is removing it from the sauvage, who claws and paws at the man's mask, trying to scrap through the layers of protection to get at the flesh inside. Seconds later, the man forgotten, it swivels its head like a mad dog, snapping and biting at the soft bits of ash floating around them like dead fireflies. For what reason it does these things, Olympe cannot fathom. The men scribble faster, and Olympe reaches into her pocket, touches her little notebook as a reminder that she'll do the same thing later, when she has the chance. There is no time now, though: the first handler is maneuvering the creature's head into Mirabelle's curved base while the executioner lowers the lunette over the top of its neck. The second handler stands at the back of the bascule, holding the creature's constantly flailing legs together with one massive hand as he keeps it against the plank with another hand flat at its back. For the first time she can recall, Olympe is revolted at the sight of so much physical corruption and decay. Black and blue discolorations entirely cover the almost skeletal body, and there are perhaps a hundred shallow and deep cuts on the creature, yet no bleeding or discharge. Her lips curl slightly—it can't be possible, but it looks as if some of the vertebrae are poking out of the skin.

And now the first handler steps back, and the executioner motions them forward. Lorilleaux and Olympe take their places, she with her copper bowl to the side, and Lorilleaux with his spidery hands reaching out to clasp the creature's jerking head. He makes a wet grunt of disgust as his fingers sink into the filthy tangle of hair and soft skin. For once, Olympe can't blame him. Everyone waits. Lorilleaux buries his nose into his shoulder and violently shudders.

She knows he's swallowing his own bile. Beneath his grip, the head keeps moving. Finally he lifts his own, and gives a single definitive nod. The sequence of events is practiced and swift. Once Lorilleaux nods, the executioner shouts out as he pulls the lever. Mirabelle's blade shoots down swift and straight, right through the creature's neck. Lorilleaux pulls the head away and holds it up for immediate inspection, while Olympe takes one step in and holds her copper bowl under the neck, catching as much of the blood as possible. As she holds the bowl, scientists will take samples from the flow, attempt to measure the rate, thickness and amount of drainage. It's all clockwork, performed perfectly by them every day without fail for three years. Nothing will go wrong.

Lorilleaux gives his nod. The executioner shouts out, and the head in Lorilleaux's grasp twists. The blade comes down and severs the neck—Lorilleaux drops the head, whipping away his hands as he shouts in pain. The head bounces down onto Olympe's feet, and instinctively, she drops her bowl and reaches down to grab it, her fingers outstretched like she's seen Lorilleaux's a thousand times. As her hands move down, the head turns: suddenly, there is pain, unlike anything she has felt before. An animal roar erupts from her throat, and she raises her arm, the head still attached, its teeth moving back and forth across her fingers like a miniature saw. She can feel the blood in her veins grow cold, the world turn black at the edges, and everything grow dull and murky and slow. Men surround her, using the calipers and any other instrument they can find to pry the horrible object from her body. And then it is over, and the head is gone. Olympe raises her hand to her face, steaming rivulets of red running down her palm and disappearing in the sleeves of her clothes. One finger is crooked, broken and almost torn in half at the knuckle. When she speaks, it's as if the timorous, child-like words are coming from any place other than her mouth.

—*I've been bit.*

Activity at the other guillotines has ceased. Olympe finds Nana at her side, guiding her across the eerily silenced courtyard to the holding rooms. Lorilleaux runs ahead, his blood-spattered boots echoing back and forth between the stone walls. The air feels too warm, and the ash, the ever-constant smell of burning flesh, the thick scratch at the back of her mouth—Olympe halts, bends over, and vomits. Bits of black spatter against her boots. A frisson of terror washes through her. Those black clots are her blood, darkened from sitting in her stomach for hours as it curdled into something else. Nana waits until she's finished, then guides her forward again, through the holding rooms and into a corner of a makeshift medical lab, where a physician is already bandaging up a sobbing Lorilleaux. He'll never be anything more than an assistant. He can't handle danger or pain. Olympe sits down, props her elbow upright against the table, and studies her finger. Already the edges of the wound are drying out, cracking slightly. Moistening a rag with her spittle, she wipes the blood away and leans in, squinting. A low moan escapes her lips, barely a feather's breath. Tiny veins of blue and black thread away from the edges of the bite marks, a network that spreads as she watches, imperceptibly slow but sure. Around the lines, the flesh blossoms in a soft pale gray. Olympe grabs a roll of clean linen and quickly begins wrapping her hand. The doctor attending Lorilleaux doesn't protest. They all know how hard she works, how quick and smart she is. Olympe takes care of herself. Several tears drop onto the cream fabric as she pins the ends tight, then rolls down her stained overcoat sleeve. She'll be fine, she tells herself as she rises from her seat, ignoring Nana's steady hand. She's going to go far.

After a few sips of water, Olympe makes her way outside and back across the courtyard to Mirabelle. Already the blood has been washed away with buckets of scalding water that sends steam curling into the air, and the remaining assistants and doctors are placing equipment into straw-filled barrows to be wheeled inside. The tracks of another wheelbarrow lead to the doors at the rear of the courtyard, where the remains will be sent first to the morgue, and then, in pieces, to other labs on other floors. Bichet and a group of the older scientists gather at the far end of the table, staring at a liquid-filled amber container set at its edge. Hair floats in the liquid like seaweed. Normally Olympe wouldn't dare approach these important men, who know her only as a pair of disembodied hands holding a blood-filled copper bowl. She sidles along the table, her uninjured hand touching the edge casually, as if it's not necessary to keep her balance. When she gets to the edge of the group, Bichet straightens, and waves her closer. The men move aside: they're making way for *her*. Little trickles of sweat run down the sides of her face. It feels like her body is pushing all the fluids out, squeezing out every last drop of moisture, to make room for the gray blossoms and the black veins.

Bichet reaches out and grabs the top of the container, twisting it around with his nimble surgeon's hands. Olympe crouches down until her chin rests on the tabletop, as though she were five again. Seaweed waves of dark hair make way for a face, bruised and contorted. The eyes are clouded over but open, and they blink, and they see Olympe. *Tête vivante*, someone whispers. Thick globs of blood stick to its lips, preserved by the fluid. Some of that blood is hers. A part of her will always be in that jar, trapped between the lips of something that is not dead or alive. The mouth opens in a soundless cry, and a piece of tooth floats out, disappearing in the waving hair. Olympe turns and runs from the table stumbling across the courtyard back to the holding rooms. Behind her, loud laughter floats and tumbles and mixes with the snowy crematory ash.

Time and the day and the ashes in the air sift past Olympe in an increasing haze of detachment and low-grade pain. She hovers near the door of the holding room, watching the handlers walk to and fro with their living cargo. None of the sauvages that they take to the guillotines are ill, as far as she can tell. Men walk back and forth between the assistants, jars and dishes and bowls filling and emptying. Heads, feet, bones, blood. A farmer's market of grotesqueries and abominations. And in the distance the fires eat away at the remains, vomiting out the bits onto their heads. She stares into the distance. Her face is somewhere else. She can't feel her lips. Everyone in the courtyard coughs, hocks, spits. Something happened today that she should be weeping about, but she can't remember. She holds up her bandaged hand. The nails are black as beaded jet. They look oddly fetching.

Light gray flakes float around and against her skin. A lone idea flares to life in her mind. It's the ash. They got sick, all of them, every person and sauvage in the building, from the airborne remains of the burning dead. Olympe shivers hot and cold with the incredible scientific significance of her thoughts. All those smart men in the building, and she alone knows. She's figured it out. Life into death, into life, into death. Ouroborus. That's what the—

Nana is helping her into her scarf and coat. Is the day over already? It feels as if she only just arrived. Beyond the doors, the courtyard is pitch black, silent until tomorrow morning when the blades spring back to life. Life. Something about life. Someone walks her through the thick double gates. His face is familiar, plump and delicious. Red wet fruit in a desert. Outside, the world is quiet and calm. She hears the muted roar of the furnace far behind her, all the machinery hidden within the building that keeps it alive to gobble up all in the name of Science. Rue St. Martin lies before her like a dried-up river, pointing a dim, insurmountable way back into Paris proper. Lights twinkle overhead in the black of night, tumble down and brush against her face. Olympe sighs. She used to remember what those are. She breathes them in as she drags her feet down the raggedy sides of the road.

A lamp post or tree trunk is at her back. When did she stop walking and sit down? The night is cold. She should feel it, but she doesn't. She should care, but.

She is going to go far.

The ash.

It was the bite, and the ash.

Olympe wills her numb fingers to begin a laborious creep through the layers of fabric, toward her notebook and pencil, though she cannot feel their progress or lack thereof. No matter, she must somehow write down her scientific observations and present them to the others in the morning, before the disease spreads further. This knowledge will be the society's salvation, its debridement, and her way out. Olympe will be taken seriously, taken under wing. Respect, at last. She will become a scholar, a doctor, a brilliant beacon of light and an example to all women of France. She stares down. Her hand is a hand that is not her hand and it is all the way on the other side of Paris or perhaps even the world and she does not know what it is at all or what it holds. At the quiet end of the street, the building stands tall and funereal against scrabbly trees and darkling sky. The river of Time rushes steadily into and through her, filling her up until all she sees and feels and hears is a great slow blanket of nothingness: and everything stops.

Disconnected images well up into her mind, images of each silky shining drop of blood out there in the dark, spurting and squirting from the bright flat mouths of open necks, and her small calloused hands and the wide bowl of her mouth to catch them all. Warm red, squirming and streaming behind the outlines of the shapes so rapidly approaching her. Bright red, to push the gray of the world away.

YOURS IS THE RIGHT TO BEGIN

1 November
Outside Bistritz
Sunset

"...darkness, lapping water, and creaking wood."

Tick, tick, tick at the end of the chain swings the watch, and back against your fireside bed of needles and furs you collapse and drift away, sweet sister Mina, your thoughts unmoored by the doctor's trick twitch of his mesmerizing wrist, your mind free to wander the wild woods, gleaning the lingering scent of your captive beloved, reporting back to that fierce, relentless Helsing demon all the secrets hidden within our master's untamed kingdom of night. Or so we make him believe.

Drip, drip, drip go the sounds of my thoughts under each little tick of the watch, each unspoken word welling plump from the dark woods and rushing waters and starry void of my mind, staining red all the untouched pink flesh of your soul. In this manner I speak to you, as did the First, who spoke to me a century ago, who plucked me like turning fruit from a long-forgotten tree.

Out there in the cold crisp dying of the sunset's flaming light you speak of inconsequential things to your doctor, visions of trails and pathways and roads unseen. Inside, your thoughts drift to the man you love, directing my desires away from your unbroken velvet neck, and yet even as your supple mouth silently wraps around his name I slip into your visions beside him, unheard and unseen, nestling like a buzz just beyond your ear, a warm vibrating hum whispering warm against the rising hairs on your skin. That flush on your pale cheek, my innocent Mina, that effervescence coursing through your blood, is that not also a pure and perfect love? Can I not give you the same?

I am the youngest. I am the Third. What the others have long forgotten, what dark centuries and the monotony of undying time have scrubbed away, I remember still. Traces in the air and against my tongue, like the remnants of a last unforgettable meal. The swelling valleys and hills of the Mittel Land, vast expanses of bright green fields under brilliant sun, the snow-capped mountains but a hazy suggestion at the horizon. Pears and cherries, hard red apples dropping to the warm earth. She came from these lands, the First told me, and to them she returned in the low mists of one early summer some half a century ago, burrowing her way through the warm brown earth, her gold hair and fair limbs entangled in the soft roots of tall grass and vegetables. There as the season quickened did she take both rest and power, soaking up the heat of the sun, small insectile life and fragile-boned burrowers that heard her lovely, low call. And above the ground, as the season ripened, we heard her silent song, and we came, too.

Rumors of a mist, sparkling like crushed stained glass, swirling around dusky plums that couples stole and ate before they sunk into the grass, into each other, into the earth itself, their bodies found at daylight, hollowed and open-eyed, dry cavities packed with sticky stems and stones. Young girls from neighboring farmlands wandering down roads in the early hours of the morning, covered in beads of dew, pale and feverish, their shaking fingers scratching at wounded necks as they asked which way was home, the words dribbling out of their split lips in slow crimson waterfalls. Mothers sleep-walking newborn babies into the fields, leaving them under the fruit trees like offerings, only days later to awaken in horror, unable to remember what they had done. Circle of cats and dogs, bloodless, beheaded and neatly arranged on the grounds of a local church cemetery. In the center of each circle a pink newborn's hand placed upright, a cold supplication, a decaying plea.

The village slipped into paralyzed silence as the summer bloated and crept toward its autumnal end, cobblestone streets emptied out, windows shuttered tight and rooms darkened, clusters of crosses and garlic swung at every door. It meant nothing. She fed on us all, and left the seeds and cores and skins of her human crop to shrivel away. I remember my father coming to me during the day, thick ropes of iron dragging from his worn, broken hands. He stopped, stared up at the ceiling, and began whispering replies at the shadowy corners to questions I never heard. Eventually he dropped the chains and left the room. I never saw him again. Outside, insects chattered and buzzed incessantly in the heat. So many creeping things, and not a single bird left to cull them. Cows dying and crops fallow in the fields, and only that one lush mound of the valley blossoming like a poison-soaked paradise, whilst all the land around it cowered and waited. Every night I dreamed, thrashing away the soaking sheets, ripping off my bedclothes. In the stifling dark, my hands crept across my body, and my brown skin was the valley, and she was there, in the center, under the folds of the earth, calling out my name, waiting for my touch. And though I held out longer than the rest, so, too, like the others in the village, I found myself drawn to her as well, making my way through a late-summer village drained of all people and life, walking through rotting and fly-blown orchards and fields in the star-studded hour before nightfall, a bouquet of dead, dried flowers in my shaking hands, flowers that exploded into life as I neared her ground, bursting with sticky pollen and green water. And there on that hill in the vast rolling Mittel Land, I, the last of my village, the last of my valley, slid my fingers inside the rich damp loam of the world, teasing her out little by little until she unfurled over me and inside me, gold wheat hair and milk skin, plum-sweet lips and a tongue of sharp, sour wine. And there was pleasure, unlike any I had ever known, wave after wave of rich red desire rising up to crash abated against my body's shores, and she pressed my head against her breasts and throat like a hungry child. And a single lap of her blood took it all forever away.

Our bodies are dead, our souls are dust, and decay cannot desire. So she says. My mind cannot forget her, though, cannot shed the memories of her on me, inside me, as she did before I was undone. Like a tickle, a silvery shiver against my skin, the maddening ghost of a touch never truly realized, a desire never fulfilled. The First floats above us in the night when our master has not allowed us out to be fed, and we, the Second and the Third, open our mouths like helpless birds. She bites her fingertips like a cat, and we catch the trickling of blood running off her sharp nails with our snapping teeth and pointed tongues, lapping up more air than sustenance. In each drop I remember the sensation of summer, the crops and fields and lap of the midday sun. I remember her tongue, the smell of the living earth on her breasts and hands. I remember, but my body is cold. I reach up for her, but she is always too far away. And I would go mad at the memory of it all, except for the blood, those few drops of thick plum from her hands that abate the hunger and pain. And so I scrabble greedily about in a cold barren room in a castle that has no name, for a few exquisite sparks of a long-lost summer. Endless winter in these mountains, endless desiccated life, two lovers, and no love at all.

Will this be your existence? Will this be you?

What is it that I say and do here in the cold, in the snow of a country that it not my home? I do not wish to know.

Full of beauty of all imaginable kinds this country is, and every woman, delicious Mina, is a country. Terrible is the country that you travel to. She reaches out to you even now, and you will live forever in a land pregnant with dead branches of desire, continually consumed in hunger's red wave. I do not think it is there that you belong. And the first tendrils of purple morning swell up through the thick trees, and I rise with them, exploding and scattering like floating seeds. Later, when you awaken, your wet clothes will still glitter with the spent remains of that which once was me.

2 November
The Carpathian Spurs
Sunrise

"...darkness, creaking wood, and roaring water."

Night swells and peaks, and still you sleep. I grimace and ride the hours with it, even to the painful razor edge of it, until dawn begins to push its way up through the thin membrane of the horizon, anxious to start the day. Only then does your good companion take out his watch, and so begins your inevitable turn on the Catherine wheel of my thoughts. I waste no time.

I am the Second. I was there at the beginning, I watched the First die and unbecome, and then she cleaved unto me and once again we were brought together in all things and through all things, I once again her willing servant ready to give her my undying life and love.

There are rules, stubborn little Mina. Just as there are rules that govern the entirety of nature, rules that dictate the passage of that water you think you hear, the swaying of those wind-blown branches you think you see, so there are rules that govern his entire world, which is this entire world. As I did, as we all did, you will become a servant to each and every one. No man or mortal shall do your unnatural bidding again. You will be Fourth, and you will drink last, never first. You will be last in everything, you will be the Least. Unbecome by her blood, you will finally learn to submit.

You must never again pay heed to the words and actions of the Third.

You must never leave our chambers unless by his command, through the First.

You must never raise your head in his presence, or look him directly in the eyes. As he is in all things above you, so in all things must you forever remain below.

You must never speak in his presence; and throughout all of the castle confines and the world itself, for all time, you must never speak, or even think, his name.

You must never mention his long-dead sons, though you will be made, as we all are, to dress in their rusting armor and place their helmets over your bound and braided hair. You must show no fear when he drags us to barren fields of skeletons and stone, and under storm-gray skies mounts us upon petrified pikes and crosses, crying out betrayers, betrayers all with every hammer blow, black gouts from your body squirting against ragged pike and steel, impaled flesh firing white-hot bolts of pain into your shrieking, shrinking soul. You must pay no heed to his laughter when the rays of a feeble morning sun curl the edges of your skin, burn wet layers of your eyes away like autumn mist. All our wounds heal, eventually.

You must not pass out when he nails your clothes to your breasts, when he drives a spike through your tongue. You must learn to lick your lips and pant for more.

In every moment of your existence, you must remember that the physical world is his domain, and no longer yours to command. By air alone, you must travel backwards and never forward, never touching ceilings or floors or walls, whether he is there to see you or not. Always you must travel with your ruby eyes seeing only where you have been, never where you are going, because your destination is nowhere. There is only the past, he says, and we must never forget it. We live forever, but for us there is no future. We are dust, and we move as such.

Books are forbidden, as is music and all the forms of the arts. You must learn to find stories in wind, knowledge in thunder and rain. Your thoughts will no longer be yours to write down, your little diaries and letters shredded and burned. Every transgression will be paid to him with a finger, which he will place in a thin glass bottle and display on our chamber walls. You are not allowed to touch these bottles or take them down. Centuries will pass, and you will gaze upon the forest of fingers you have lost and regrown and lost again, ageless and perfectly preserved in their transparent reliquaries. Unnecessary, useless, broken, replaceable. You will learn that this is us. This will be you.

Once a year, he will dress you in the remnants of a four-hundred-year-old gown, lead you backwards up broken stairs, floating over toothless gaps in the stone, until you find yourself in the highest crooked tower, perched over the deepest ravine in the Carpathians, staring half a mountain's length down to a river so ageless and relentless and hard it has split the very heart of the land in half, never to be whole again. You must not resist his spider-hard grasp at the small of your back as he sends you flying over the edge, nor must you allow your flailing limbs to claw for purchase as you plummet unstoppable into the ravine's crooked maw, bones breaking and snapping with every outcrop of jagged rock. He will fly with you, twisting and turning with every spiral of your breaking body, fingers grasping your neck as he watches all the moments of your life rise and fall like oily tides on your grimacing visage. Do not ask what it is he looks for, what undiscovered truths he seeks in the dark calligraphy of tears penned by your horrified eyes. The ice-black currents will not stop or slow your descent, only push your ribs up through breaking skin like snowy mountain peaks, red mist rising from your body like a distant summer dawn. And when the raging waves vomit your ravaged body from their foamy grip, you will not plead for death or mercy as he rearranges the wet velvet folds of your gown against the iron shores, whispers in your ear the name of a woman you do not know, then leaves your split corpse to gather the first feathers of midnight snow.

And I will come for you, gentle, broken, fearless Mina, as I came for the First so many centuries ago, when I witnessed her fall, the first fall. I will collect your body and carry you backwards all the way, backwards and up through crevices and caverns and passages, no guide except all the ghosts of my former journeys through lost centuries, the worn grooves in the packed earth, the smooth hollows in the stones. And to our chambers I will deliver you, and outside the thick castle walls seasons will pass and change as we lick your wounds and the ivory of our teeth clicks against the white of your ribs, pushing the destruction back inside, back down. Our lips against yours, hot kisses in the darkness, fingers crawling and stitching, swollen folds of flesh closing and opening, the wet of our blood and desire a crucible to transmute and banish all pain: until the following year, when he throws you off the tower once again. And he will be there, at all times watching over all your deaths and rebirths, because all that you do will be for him. All that you experience will be his, over and over, for all eternity.

You must break, and you must heal, and you must break, and you must heal. Sisyphus, never resting at the summit. Icarus, never reaching the opposite shore.

Is this you, pretty finger in a jar? Will this be you?

Except. I feel it on your breath, against the rigid curve of your spine, in the beat of your steady heart behind such cold, small breasts. There is nothing wax about you. And the watch on its chain slows and stops, and you slip away, toward the mysterious country of daylight I can no longer travel through. And night flows on across the mountains, dragging with it the ominous grays of another relentless day, indistinguishable from any other before it, or after.

3 November
Borgo Pass
Sunrise

"…darkness and the swirling of water."

Those glass-cased fingers embedded in the castle walls, Mina: they are not hers. Flesh of my flesh, each one severed from my hands. A forest of defiance and insurrection, thousands of markers pointing every way in every direction, proclaiming at once, I am everywhere, and here. He catches me looking at them, running my newly grown fingers over the filthy vials, pinpricks of blood coalescing in my eyes. He mistakes the look on my face for sorrow, for resignation, for ruin. Everywhere men are surrounded by life, and see it not at all. Malformed, grotesque monstrosity, he drags his loathsome remains to the center of the web and thinks himself safe as he hallucinates away his years, dreams and schemes of his former self made whole, an immortal conqueror striding across an impaled and broken world as he blots out the sun with the crimson letters of the ancient, unspeakable First Name.

He does not realize the name he writes is mine.

"This is the way."

4 November
Borgo Pass
The Red of the Dawn

"Why fear for me? None safer in all the world from them than I am."

In the blissful black silence of the woods, beneath the hiss of wind and snow, you hear them. The faint suck and suction of their mouths, the swift rush of life down their transparent throats, the soft sighs of steam rising off the fallen horses entwined in their smooth brown arms. Life: never extinguished, simply traveling, from one perfect creation to the next. Pale flakes drift up around the undead and the dying, all of them heedless to the rising drifts, the pressing cold. Stars wheel and gyre mindlessly in the heavens above us. Branches dislodge their heavy wintery burden, anointing the heads of wolves with silver crowns. And all the terrors of the night have vanished, valiant Mina, deep into the obsidian oblivion of a sudden sleep. Is this not the most beautiful of all countries? Is this not the most wondrous of all nights?

Twice have I come to you in the valleys and mountains of this kingdom, moving the mindless bodies of the Second and the Third as the rosemary honey of my words poured from their puppet mouths. Twice have I watched as you stood trembling but resolute, and refused. Trails of salty blood now crack and flake against my sister's cheeks, yet already they no longer remember that less than a winter's breath ago, they gnashed their teeth at you a third time, wept and rent their garments and breasts as they screamed. That is who they are, and what you might have become. No less animal than the helpless animals they now suckle at, no less mindless in their destruction like winter storms. They speak and spin stories of such aching beauty and pain, yet the words and emotions that pour from their fang-tipped mouths, the shifting forms of their flesh, the touch of their pliant hands are mere traps to catch flies. Bereft of me inside, their actions are nothing but the hunger, taking what revolting shapes and sounds it needs, the quicker to fell the prey, the quicker to feed. They forget what they are, what they used to be. United in infinite confusion and pain, they exist as much on blood as the ever-changing fantasies of what I tell them their meaningless lives could have been, could still be.

To the Third I came in the dregs of a plague-laced summer, the crops and animals already long dead, the villages of that distant valley festering under disease and endless sun. I imbued and impregnated the overworked earth with the corruption of my presence, and rose from flies and fumes hissing from poisoned ground, from slick green ropes of mossy decay bubbling from stagnant pools. I lingered in the blackening veins and mottled skin of all living creatures who lapped and nibbled away at the fruits and flowers and leaves of my sweet false call. A vegetable husk of life she was when the Third succumbed to my song, when she dragged her withered breasts and brittle bones across the soft black pulp of her lands and family to fall apart in my arms, aching for release. Death alone is release. My embrace gives none.

To the Second I came in the mirror shards of soured celestial visions, an iron maiden angel born from the fevered blood mists of suppressed perversions and misplaced belief. Beneath the revolting excess of vaulted stone ceilings, golden crucifixes and diamond-studded monstrances, far below the scratching swirl of incense, the smoke of white wax and blue flame, under layer upon layer of monotone, miserable lives lived in fealty to a long-dead god, I burrowed up from pagan foundations and writhed against crumbling mosaics, feeding on plump, lost novices and fucking ossified bones as I howled my song of songs. It was there she crawled to me, whip-lashed and pierced, begging for my mortification of her sin-choked, naked flesh, begging for a pain-filled path to a virgin monstrosity. And under the unblinking watch of the skull-studded ceilings and walls did I eat the lids off her wondering eyes, and reveal the darkness and emptiness of faith, the vast insignificance of the human soul, forever in the cosmos falling and alone.

And at the last, undisguised by guile and sorrows and dreams, I come to you. I am the First and am in all things the First, which is my eternal right. I alone bestowed that power and privilege upon myself a hundred hard lifetimes ago, and no man or creature fashioned or forged me. I am a creature of my own making, as all women are. Even to him, I was the First, making him who he was, though he no longer remembers and has usurped my place, re-written his history and calls himself my Master. And yet even this betrayal shall eventually serve me, for I tell truths to few women, and to no men. I am the Queen of Lies. I live and breathe in the black cracks of doubt and terror that spread vast and malignant throughout all life. I am the mother of flesh rebirthed beyond perfection; I am the devouring furnace of the soul.

The low horrid laugh of my sisters, moving slow against the silence and cold. Satiated, content for an eye-blink moment of time, they drift up, float and dance with the thinning flakes of snow. I feel them at the corners of my mind, casting about for me, heads swiveling for a glance of a presence they have always known yet have never truly seen. You see me, Mina. You see me and you do not look away. The cosmic motes of my incorporeal being slide through your clothes, rippling over the curves of your cream skin, curled hair, warm lips. You breathe me in, and I stream past the hot crimson slick of your tongue into the velvet chambers of your heart, settle against and under the most secret curves of your swelling flesh. Searching, rushing through the hot motes of blood, riding the tender trembling contractions of muscles and lungs, drawing out one lingering, delicate contraction of pleasure after another and mining it for purchase. There are vast pristine skies within here, colors and landscapes and light I have not seen for centuries, achingly full with memory and promise. I could live in you for lifetime after lifetime until the heavens bled stars, and never feed. In you, I have no need to be First. I have no purchase. In you I am contentment, nothingness, alone.

The only darkness within you, inviolate Mina, is me.

Outside our bodies, outside of dreams and sleep, the beautiful sun is breaking across the jagged mountains, golden light creeping through slender trees and sparkling snow. Streams and strands of me pour like the morning mists from your limbs, minute shards of ice that settle against the branches, burn away. Later you will wake, you will rise, you will turn your face upward into the light of a world that is the mirror of your soul, and you will continue your descent into my kingdom, swelling like the great and gentle ocean until there is no more darkness, no more water, no more lies and dreams. Until only you remain, and your right to begin.

Come to me.

LORD OF THE HUNT

Every slow Sunday a woman named Connie wanders the Tacoma Mall, searching for something she's never found: the last thing she'll ever desire. She's lighter than dust, with a hole in her heart the size of her nameless hunger. Connie sifts through sequined racks of silk, strokes gold-capped columns of perfumes. Glittering makeup stains her fingers, necklaces slide through her hands. Her breath mists display glass as mannequins pose, sloe-eyed, silent and unmoved. Connie is unmoved. Each bright bauble only leads to another, only whispers of better things. She wants the clasp and chain of all possessions, she wants to feel the weight of want's end. As always, Connie drifts in disappointment, down to the very last store.

It's sat there for decades, a musty emporium, looking as if the mall had been built around it. Medieval armor stands guard at the entrance, heralding the presence of fake antiques crammed inside. Connie enters, tobacco and cedar scents biting at her eyes. She fondles scrimshaw pipes and chess sets, examines lighters etched with Celtic symbols and feathered Tlingit masks. Worn pastorals carved into sideboards gather dust, goats and shepherds cavort in gilded frames. They stare out at her, past her with hollowed eyes, and she past them, hollowed. Connie sees them every time. Usually nothing changes.

Usually.

The statue crouches in a grime-covered cabinet, partially hidden behind a cracked crystal ball. She points to it, casual in movement. Nothing to get excited over, she just hasn't seen it before. The old man unlocks the case, grasps the bronze creature with tissue-paper hands. He drops it on the counter. The glass groans. Connie sighs.

A god stands before her: muscular legs, barrel chest, the hirsute face of a devil, masculine and strong. Antlers jut past sharp ears, a crown of tangled bone pierces the air above him. Connie runs a finger through the horns, over the chest down to his phallus, erect between fur-coated thighs. One fingertip catches a rough edge of metal, and her hand snaps away in quick pain. In silence she reads the phrase carved on the base, her cut finger wrapped in her mouth.

CERNUNNOS
LORD OF THE HUNT

"How much," she asks.

"Well, you see, it's one of a kind." His voice washes over her, tremulous and soft, as he turns the worn price tag away. "I'm not even sure I could part with it."

"I understand." She does understand. Connie stares into the face of the creature, noting each weathered line. She sees how delicately the artist carved each vein in the arms, how the metal was ticked a million times over till the antlers seem coated in velvet. How could anyone part from him? How could anyone want for anything, after possessing him? Connie licks her lips. Her feet shift as hot blood pumps and plummets between her thighs.

"I couldn't afford it, I'm sure," she mutters.

"Oh, if you want something bad enough, you find a way to pay."

Connie half-listens. She stares at the statue as she licks her wound. Blood wells at the phallus tip, then disappears. Connie squints.

Does the metal swell, move? Does the chest stretch, inhale? Does his cock quiver?

Connie quivers.

"I have ten thousand dollars." The words drop out of her, unbidden. It's true, she has a savings account, of sorts—bits of metal scrounged over the years, rolled and rubber-banded, handed to a smirking teller at the end of each working week. Her only cushion for the oubliette of a lonely future she's been falling toward for years. Money for pills and pabulum, bedpans and the grave.

The old man shrugs. From hidden corners of the store, someone laughs, and branches scrape soft against cabinets. "That's a lot of money to be carrying around. Are you sure you have that much?"

"I can give you a cashier's check. I just need to go to the bank—there's a branch in the mall. Please."

"It's not much. What's ten thousand dollars, anyway, if you can throw it away like—" The old man shakes his hands. Dry leaves pinwheel down the aisles, gather in whispering clumps by the counter. Connie mashes them against her soles, grinding them into the floor.

"Please. I *want* this." Her hand steals over his, light as her whisper. Her fingertips move in neat circles on his skin. What is she doing?

He blushes and lowers his head. Connie wonders—has a woman ever looked at him, ever touched him like this? How would it feel, to be swept into such antediluvian emotion, to feel the bright rush of lust at the end of life, knowing only the void of dark will ever follow?

This is what I want to know.

"Well. Come back at closing. I'll clean the statue for you." He pats her hand, grandfatherly, and moves it away. Connie smiles, ashamed. She murmurs her thanks, stumbles out of the store. In five hours, Cernunnos will be hers.

"Victory," she says, as it quickens inside.

About her, pale mannequins smile.

***

Fading sunlight follows Connie as she rushes through the mall, damp fingers clutching an envelope. As she moves down the halls, security gates lower, cutting off protests of lingering wanderers. But all stores must close, as all days must end, even the longest of the year. Solstice, Connie remembers. After today, everything falls toward fall like a lover's last embrace.

The emporium door is shut, the lights are dimmed. Cupping her hands, Connie presses against the window and peers inside. No movement, no man, no statue. Did he change his mind? She knocks hard against the glass, pain nipping her knuckles. From within, a muffled voice speaks, and she shouts, "I said I'd be back, let me in!" The high ceilings echo her excitement, as if invisible flocks of harpies ride the stale air. Calm down, she tells herself, as the old man opens the door.

"Here." She thrusts the envelope at him, and he takes it, juggling keys as he locks the door behind her. "Ten thousand dollars. Cashier's check. Like I promised." Her voice is rich and throaty, coated with longing. She used to speak like that all the time. That was forty years, half a lifetime, ago.

"Yes, like you promised." The old man stares at the envelope, nods his head. "I cleaned it up for you, it's in the back. But I can't find the box it came in. Let me go and look around again."

"No!" Connie winces at her sharpness, starts over again. "It's all right, I don't need the box. I can put it in my bag."

The old man frowns. "Those antlers will tear your pretty purse right up. Sit down, relax. I'll be just a minute." He walks to the back of the narrow shop, vanishes behind a door. Connie leans against the counter, thinks about antlers tearing, carving maps into mysterious leather lands. Her head bows down, rests against cool glass. Her future is gone. All she has is this feeling clotting up her heart, ripe and ready to burst. Her eyelids close. Behind them, forests rise.

***

Howls, full-throated and lush, roll through the woods with the rushing wind. Connie starts, elbows sliding off the counter as she opens her 'eyes. Overhead, mechanical ticking has replaced the rustling of leaves.

The time. Connie bolts upright, stares at the clock. In the dim gloom, the hands relentlessly eat the seconds away. She gasps, laughs a little, horrified. It's just past eight. She'd fallen asleep, wandered in the woods, for three full hours.

"Hello?" Connie calls out, tentative. Beyond the drone of the clock, silence crouches and waits. She steps away from the counter, searching for a glimpse of light. Her fingertips stay at the counter's edge, ensuring the rest of her doesn't drift away. At the far end of a row of armoires, the wooden door stands silent, no light shining from behind. The old man has vanished, and with him, the statue. Her fingers spasm into fists as they remember the warmth of the metal, the heaviness of her longing. A prick at her finger was all it took.

Connie slips off her jacket and shoes, lets her purse fall to the floor. As her hands drop the strap, they slide up her waist, cup her breasts and squeeze. The weight of her flesh grounds her. She arches her back, stretches up and out, dispels the last of sleep, moves forward. She's paid the price, paid for years. She's not leaving without him.

The knob turns easily under her grasp, the door swings soundlessly open. Rows of metal shelves rise to the ceiling, crammed with boxes and crates. Connie's heels click against concrete, carry her past cobwebbed weaponry, boxes of spiced snuff. Overhead, a single bulb casts out a sickly glow, barely visible. She grabs the chain and flicks it off. "Better," she whispers.

From ahead and below, a wet grunt breeches the dark. Connie freezes, hands to mouth. The sound has a greedy, longing tone.

She drops to a crouch and sniffs the flowing air. Musky, copper-cold.

Connie sidles to the end of the aisle. Against the wall, on a worktable, tools and dust cloths lay scattered under rivulets of blood. Her eyes follow the spray, up— Droplets fall from the ceiling, and she licks her lips, recognizing the taste. Strips of bronze, melted and curved, smoke at her feet. She flips over a piece, reads the half-word:

CERNUN

He's free.

"Not for long. I'll find you," Connie vows, with lips sweat-salted plump. To the left, another corridor, an open door. Red hoof prints point the way. She follows the wide pattern, ghosting his wake. Shelves give way to furniture, crammed in layers like abandoned centuries. Dressers drip with carvings, armchair gargoyles tongue the air. Beyond the opening, concrete dissolves under dirt and scrub. Further beyond, from out of the cavernous black, a distant, mournful howl. Connie hesitates. Everything looks bigger in the next room, wider and wilder. How will she find him in that vast space? How will she carry him back?

What if I don't need to?

Snuffling—the rustle of animals from behind, of fur-lined limbs weaving through table legs. Connie slips through the door, locks it tight, and enters a warehouse of forever. Crumbling mausoleums and statues line cracked roads, furniture perches on barrows and plateaus. Just past the road, wood-slatted shacks and houses lean against each other, yellowing price tags hanging off doorknobs. Connie looks to the horizon as she walks, to jagged mountains covered in ruined buildings. Fluorescent lights dangle from bare branches, casting shadows over obelisks. She notes how the cords hang upward, as if gathering the light from a sky crammed full of stars. Bright flashes draw her to banks of cabinets half-sunk in the ground. Connie gasps in pleasure at the sight of jewel-crusted creatures and blinking marble busts, resting on rippling velvets. All the antiquities of the world are here, all the mysteries, all the desires. All the things she's searched for, that she once would have loved. They're not enough, not now.

At the end of the banks, three roads fork out from the one. A dog lies in the middle road, gutted and scattered. Connie follows his serpentined entrails into a narrow valley crowded with long-forgotten gods, sleeping and marked down for sale. Alabaster spiders spin webs over limbs of cerulean, muting the blue with needle-thin shards of silver. Wolves race past her now, boars and beasts—Connie jumps into the crook of an indigo goddess as an auroch thunders past, hooves pounding half-circles into the ground. Challengers, all answering the call of their lord.

Rising from the goddess, she follows them, follows sounds and scents of battle and death. Ahead, another fork. Down the right path, fat columns cluster and shine in moonlight, flanking travertine buildings. A price tag flutters from a post. Connie plucks it out of the wind, and reads:

LIBRARY, ALEXANDRIA
INQUIRE AT REGISTER FOR PRICE

The left-hand path leads into trees, the largest she's ever seen. Hulking colossi thrust from the earth, branches brushing the ground like unbound hair. No stars or fire here, no sign or sight of man. Only blood mist of the dying, the hard light of the moon, and the guttural breath of a warrior, as he waits.

Connie drops the tag and takes the left path, her hand on her heart. Heaviness blossoms, spreads dark-stained lust through her limbs like blood in water. She thickens. Bones crunch under her feet, animals shudder, release death rattles into cold air. Another time, another place, she would have cowered and wept. This is not another time, another place. This is the only time, the only place.

There has never been anything else.

He stands in the center of a clearing, alive and hot-blooded, magic pumping hard under oily bronzed skin. Thick muscles flex beneath coils of brown hair, tumid curves of flesh swing between his legs. A feral face turns to her—not human or demon but something of both, sharp and sensual. Bloodied mouth, and eyes like slivers of gold. At the end of his grasp lies the auroch, its life jetting out in rivers around their feet.

Come to me, she would say, if she could speak. *Be with me. Be with me.* But language does not belong here, no longer exists. Her tears spell his name on her skin. Connie steps into the clearing, arms out. He moves back, dissolves into shadowed trees, and disappears. Night winds rush through the forest, and needled branches buckle and crack, filling the air with ozone and evergreen. Connie stands, awe-struck and uncertain, warm ground beneath her feet. She came for him, but how can she tear him away from such desolate beauty? How can she tear herself?

The trees give no reply.

Connie's hands move from button to button, parting the fabric of her blouse. Her skirt slides down in a silken whoosh to the ground. She sheds her clothes like unwanted skin, and walks to the center of the clearing, shivering in pleasure. Her body hasn't felt the naked air in decades. Arms raised, Connie stares up at obsidian night, endless and terrible. Unbearable: unless she opens herself, unless she lets herself drown.

This is what I want to know.

Dark earth lifts as she lowers herself, dark earth cradles her spine. It displays her hair, her breasts, her limbs in the up-thrust language of love. She is desire, the chthonic void, the true endless O of night that the horned god might bow down to, might enter and rest in her deepness, eternally loved.

And He does; and He does.

*** *

Every slow Sunday, a young girl named Josie wanders the wide corridors of the Tacoma Mall. She tries on clothes she can't afford, carves her name into furniture displays. Stolen earrings slip into her pockets, purloined chocolates slide into her mouth. Lately she's followed young mothers around, staring at fat babies cradled in arms. She cradles herself and feels nothing. She wants weight, she craves substance and purpose. Usually she never finds it.

Usually.

She sees the statue in the emporium, in the cabinet over the counter. Josie fingers the lighters, the yellowing pipes: but the statue catches her heart. The old man lifts it, carefully places it down on the counter before her. Josie wipes her eyes.

A goddess of gold, stag-horned and heavy, squats on a pedestal. Large breasts rest against a stomach bulging with child, hair drapes her shoulders in velvety waves. Wide mouth, wild eyes. Josie cups the statue's stomach, rests a finger in the groove between her legs. She feels warmth, wetness, the slow beat of two hearts. Josie's eyelids flutter and close. She feels her deepness.

Josie smiles and opens her eyes, speaks with a lover's full sigh.

"How much."

IN THE COURT OF KING CUPRESSACEAE, 1982

OCTOBER 23: A DARK WAVE DANCE AT THE COMMAND OF YOUR KING
THE VOIDOIDS. ALIEN SEX FIEND. ⬡●◆♎⬡♎⬡ BLACK FLAG.
FALCO. THE POLICE. GARY NUMAN. VIOLENT FEMMES. YAZOO.
LENE LOVICH. ♏○⊠♏⬡ THE DEAD KENNEDYS. MINISTRY. THE
DAMMED. STIMULATORS. EURYTHMICS. ⬡●◆♎◆ THE CLASH.
♎●◆⬡♎◆♏□⚹◆□ BUZZCOCKS. THE. SLITS. NOMI. SEX PIS-
TOLS. ⬡⤢●⬡ SIOUXSIE AND THE BANSHEES. BLONDIE. THE
POLICE. SPLIT ENZ. ROMEO VOID. ELVIS COSTELLO. NINA HAGEN.
THE VISIBLE TARGETS. BAUHAUS. B-MOVIE. VISAGE. PETE SHELLEY.
ENGLISH BEAT. SHRIEKBACK. ♋◆⬡♎⚹◆□♋●◆⬡♎ THE VA-
PORS. XTC. YELLO. THE SPOONS. ⬡◆♒⬡♎●⬡ THE SMITHS.
DAVID BOWIE. TOTO COELO. THE MOTORS. ●♎⬡□◆♏ NEW
ORDER. OINGO BOINGO. JOY DIVISION. ●⬡♎□ WALL OF VOO-
DOO. B-52'S. THE BEAT. ♎⌘⌘⌘⌘ GENERATION X. KING CRIMSON.
GANG OF FOUR. □◆◆□♏■▭ ◆●⬡♎◆ THE FLESHTONES. THE
FIXX. PATTI SMITH. ♎⬡ ●♒▭◆●♎◆◆□◆ HAYSI FANTAYZEE.
THE CRAMPS. THE CARS. ULTRAVOX. BUTTHOLE SURFERS. TEARS
FOR FEARS. ◆◆□□♏ FLYING LIZARDS. X-RAY SPEX. GO4. THE STY-
RENES. ■♋▭●⬡♎♒♒ ⬡◆◆●◆⬡◆♒⬡♎●⬡ ♎⬡♎⌘●⬡
DEVO. GRACE JONES. MC5. THE THE. ART OF NOISE. TELEVISION.
DEPECHE MODE. ♋⬡▭□◆ ◆□♏♎⬡⬡♎♎♎◆♏♎⬡⬡◆♎

67

INXS. THE FALL. ⸮&□◆ ⸮&ℯ□◆ ⚏ℯ℈ BRONKSI BEAT. OIN-
GO BOINGO. ⚏□ℯ℔◆⸌⚏⚶○□℔&●&⚏ ⸮⊠&ℯ ⚏□◆⤳▪
&●⸮&⚏◆℔ ⤳ &●⚏⤶□⸌⚏ ⚏⸌□◆⚏&⤳◆● □⸌
●&○⚏ &⸮& ℔⚏&&⚏℔⚏⸮&&⸮⸌⚏ &●⚏⤶□⸌⚏⸮⊠&
903 BAYVIEW STREET. AT THE NORTHERN EDGE OF SEHOME. 11PM.⤳
⚏●◆□⸌□ DEAD OR ALIVE. ⚏⸮& ⤶□℔⚍&ℯ ⤳⚏□⸌◆℔

***

Knox and Severin stand in front of the mirror, outlining their lips
with black pencils. They are not the ordinary pencils from the sad
makeup section at the local supermarket—Knox bought these at
the store only he is able to travel to, no matter how many times
Severin follows him, only to find herself alone on the flat suburban streets of Bellingham, alone and lost under the silver sky.
Knox colors his lips in with the pencil as well, filling every plump
red fold with layers of waxy black, black to compliment the black
and gold-specked powder circling his fern green eyes. Severin fills
her lips in with a cobalt blue, the intense blue she sometimes sees
as the sun sets over the silver bay and the far Western range, the
blue that wells up out of the nothingness that occurs between the
rising of the day and the ebbing of the night, that strange and
timeless hour when the entire planet seems transported to some
ancient universe without light or heat or stars. In her tiny dorm
room bathroom, under the bright buzz of florescent tubes, Knox
and Severin silently draw. When they finish, they stare into the
mirror, at themselves, at each other. Severin flicks off the light
switch. The tiny room plunges into darkness, but their reflections
remain bright in the silver glass, skin like pale moths, hair like
flame, eyes like fireflies. Slender green threads of electricity travel
up and down the spikes of their mohawked heads. Knox turns to
her: their tongues touch tip to tip, briefly, and small sparks arc out
from their blackened fingernails, leaving feathery singe marks on
the yellowing countertop.

In the other room, Severin's roommate lies still as death under her bedcover, eyelids closed shut, hands against her mouth, pretending to sleep. Tomorrow morning, as always, she will pretend she does not remember how they sounded as they floated through the room, the long laces of their boot-clad feet making faint scratching sounds against the polished concrete floor. She will pretend she did not slip the blankets from her head after they slowly bled like grey candle smoke under the crack of the door, did not creep to the window and carefully pull back one edge of the curtain ever so slightly, did not feel the pupil of her right eye blossom wide in fright as she caught glimpses of them fluttering and winding their way four stories down through the thick trees onto the needle-covered dirt road that serpentines through the dorm complex. She will pretend she did not hear their laughter, rising with the wind. She will pretend she does not see how her glossy blonde hair grows whiter and duller with each passing day.

Later in the evening, after the show is over, Knox and Severin stand outside the club, violet-scented clove cigarettes burning down in their hands as they watch everyone else stream out, prancing like drugged werewolves down the empty 2am streets, howling and smashing empty bottles against brick walls and blacktop before melting away into the crevices of downtown Bellingham. The autumn air is chilly, and a recent sheen of rain coats everything, glistening and alive under the street lamps and buzzing neon signs. To the south, the lights of the university nestle and shine just below the dark slick of forest that blankets the massive hill behind the campus. One of those lights might be coming from Severin's dorm window, but she can't know for sure. From down here, in the misty night, it's all just a pale yellow smear, like phosphorescent mold seeping out of the earth.

Severin walks into the middle of the street, spins in a series of slow circles, leaving behind bioluminescent spirals that hold their shape in the air despite the brisk wind. It doesn't matter. No matter where she travels, she feels the links of her life leading all the way across the city and back to that room in a never-ending chain of ugly and mundane human obligations—homework, grades, unpaid bills, unanswered messages from parents and friends. It tugs at her neck like a leash and her cobalt lips grow cold—but here, with Knox, in the night, the links are somewhat weaker. Here, even in the midst of rows of blank and soulless box buildings, she feels a greater pull, up and away from the endless tangle of telephone wires that always mar her view of the limitless skies above. A pull toward what, however, she has never been able to say. She simply knows it's out there, watching, waiting. She knows Knox feels it—he's a part of it. And his mysterious ways flow from him into her, his generosity covers and enters her in spark and cold flame. At his side she can see the world and travel through it as he does. But when he fills her up until it wells out of her like pyroclastic plumes, what she feels calling her is not him.

"Now what," Knox says, two steps behind, walking through her glittering wake as she meanders down the street. His left hand is at his waist, slender fingers unconsciously looping around the bands of black leather at his waist, tapping, tapping just above the thick curve of his jeans. Perhaps consciously. He's done it too many times not to know that Severin knows what that means, how to respond, what she receives in return. She drops her cigarette to the ground and slides it across the pavement with the sole of her boot, then sidles over, pressing her crotch against his thigh as she wraps her arm around his waist, her hand gently gripping his ass. He smells like smoke and warm booze, the lingering remains of cedar oil, burnt wax and unspent spells. Severin reaches into her jacket pocket and pulls out a crumpled flier.

Knox sighs.

"No, wait. This one is different." She slips her arm away and unfolds the flier. A delicate ink outline of a gable-roofed house decorates the bottom of the flier, flanked on either side by tall evergreens that travel up the long sides. The middle of the page is crammed with tiny block letters, name after name of bands all forming a monolithic block that hovers over the house like a descending celestial fist.

"You're right. This one *is* different. They won't let you in."

"But with you."

"The other houses were more…lenient. This house, this court, is not."

Severin wants to say, *so they wouldn't let you in either,* but she keeps it to herself. She doesn't know. She knows nothing about this man. Except that he's not a man.

They reach the corner of Forest and Chestnut, and Severin pauses in the middle of the intersection. If cars pass by them, pass through them, they cannot tell. They travel slightly beside time and not in it. Knox takes a step toward Forest, which leads back toward the campus. Severin looks up past the intersection to the point in the dark where Chestnut disappears, curves, and becomes Bayview.

"There'll be other nights, Severin. Let this one go. It's not for us."

"Not even if we just stood in the yard?"

"I could come inside you for a thousand years, and it wouldn't be enough."

Severin stares at him. Her breasts strain against her fishnet top, the gold-dusted nipples poking out. Slowly her hand brushes down the front of her plaid kilt, and lifts it, past the tops of her torn stockings and the tight elastic garters, up past the thick black V of her fur. She runs her fingers through the tight curls, pulls the hair forward, and releases it. Red wet flickers of light flare up and gather around her hair, nestling, illuminating. Knox sighs again, deeper and longer, his hand moving down the hard length of his crotch.

"Take me to the house. We don't need to go inside. I just want to see." She steps back, and Knox moves forward. She feels his presence push out, push up against her, running itself up her legs and pooling in the wet folds of her aching flesh. His mysterious ways.

She takes another step back, unpinning her kilt and letting it drop to the wet ground. It will make its way back to her before the end of the night. She turns around and begins walking up Chestnut, her bare ass illuminated by the sodium street lights, by the strange light of her desire.

"Take me to the house."

"We weren't invited."

"It's a flier."

"A flier that wasn't intended for us."

"We'll stand on the other side of the street. They won't be able to do a thing."

"No."

Severin turns, purses her cobalt lips tight together, and pops them open. Her mouth is a lava tube O of dark red fire, embers rising up out of her throat and catching in the high peaks of her hair, along with her high-pitched banshee scream.

She runs along the streets, up the cracked and weed-clogged sidewalks, her thin legs pumping back and forth, hands balled up into tight fists, nails digging bloody moons into her palms. She screams and stumbles, crashes through bushes and brush, dashes along the tops of cars, then slows, turns back and looks. Knox is a tiny dot at the end of a shining asphalt line. She speeds up again, rounding the corner just as he rises in the air, body changing into what it is she has never seen, but it is fast and it is relentless and it loves to pursue her more than she loves to be chased, and now she is truly frightened because there is that moment when he catches her and she cannot quite be certain he remembers who she is and what dreamlike emotions from that other world he inhabits that alien other world which is her world might prevent him from devouring her with all of his needle thin teeth in all those mouths she catches quick glimpses of as they click and slide back in and out of other times and now she is animal running racing in the dark under stars under moons the great raging beast just behind her now in the wind at her back in the brush of the branches as they bend toward her in the uplift of the earth as she races up the low long slope of hill a worn road that leads directly to the edge of the forest the great forest the deep forest the forest that hovers high over all of the city watching and waiting and taking and an ephemeral hand is at her throat, and her legs kick out and away and she's crashing onto the ground.

Blackness and motion and air eddy and gyre around her, and within the currents Severin sees the shape of her lover's body gorging and engorging itself on her fear, forging itself into a suggestion of the being she loves. She rolls over onto her knees and crouches, shaking, her hands and elbows bruised and bloody, bits of gravel and dirt ground in with the flesh. Later, in the cool pale hours of morning, even though she'll be able to heal herself, Knox will lick her body until no trace of the wounds remains. Severin slips her jacket off—she is nothing but marble flesh covered in the transparent black remnants of clothing, bleeding and gasping for breath, her mouth and cunt twin furnaces of magic and desire. Ghostly fingers run across the outline of her jaw, touch her lips. She opens her mouth again, tears streaming down her face. She can see the bright light pouring out from her lips, feel the flesh twist and coil around in endless spirals. Out of the smoke and flame before her Knox takes full shape: legs that end somewhere in the pillars of clouds that float far beyond the edges of the Milky Way, torso and multiple arms that extend back in time to all the moments of creation large and small, a faceless head with horns that pierce the stars and move them through the skies. Severin leans forward. Out of the roiling black, it emerges: thick, wet, pulsing with veins of what she knows could not be fire. Viscous drops of light drip slowly from its rounded tip—Severin catches one with her tongue, then a second, letting her hot flesh gently flick away. She hears him moan, a long and deep rumble that sounds like the wind rushing down from the ancient mountains—he shifts, and his cock presses against her open lips, but he does not force himself. He never has. In calmer moments, Severin pretends this is his equivalent of a declaration of love.

And now Severin bends forward again, her burning mouth sliding around and down the great shaft. She cannot describe in her
human language how it feels, to be so transformed, a hollowed-out
girl reformed into fire, filling herself with the crippling desire of
an unfathomable and vast being who moves through the human
world as a strange skinny boy. She closes her eyes, but the heat
from her own body burns the lashes away, and then the lids. There
is never pain, but it frightens her nonetheless; and she clamps
down harder, locking her jaw as her mouth rotates in hard wet
circles around his flesh, as he pumps harder and faster, until they
are an engine, a blur, a storm.

He comes. It's an explosion inside her—thick gouts of magic
pouring from his cock into her throat, spreading through her body
like wildfire, burning away every centimeter of her humanity and
fashioning her briefly into something else. Above her, on another
plane of existence, Knox is screaming. Severin knows she screams
with him, but hers is primal, cellular, atomic.

She feels him slip away, out of her mouth, trailing sticky threads
of semen that hang off her bruised lips and burn away in the air.
The winds around them grow cold again, and all the little nagging
reminders of humanity come rushing in to fill Knox's absence—
her aching legs, her stiff back, her numb face. He shudders, grows
smaller, brighter, and appears before her again a contained, beautiful young man, naked and dripping with sweat. A light rain pat-
ters down. Severin tries to blink the drops away, then remembers.
She places her hands just over her eyes, concentrating. Strange
how thinking a thing can make it happen. Blinking her blindness
away, she reaches out. Knox grabs her hand and pulls her to her
feet. He always does. And then he always moves away, for a while.
This is always how it is. Is he embarrassed? Repulsed? She'll never
ask, so she'll never know.

They stand at the end of a narrow residential street. Small wood-
en houses sit on either side of them, nestled in between clumps of

gigantic firs. This is the edge of Sehome, the great untouched forest that rules from the center of Bellingham. Severin looks down
the street. From here, she sees the shimmering metallic smear of
downtown and the smoking jumble of paper mills, the bay curving like a lidless blue-black eye, and the great war of trees and human dreams—rigid roads and rows of houses slashing out against
unyielding legions of Pinopsida. This war has been won in other
cities, but not in Bellingham. And around them all floats the jagged grin of mountains, the endless unblemished arc of the sky.

"No telephone wires," she croaks. "No wires."

She led him right to it, led him with his unthinking cock. This
is her mysterious way.

Across the street, lights wink on and off and on. Small and
multi-colored, like fireflies rising up in clouds from the thick
grass. An upstairs window, apple-round, glows soft pink. And
then the downstairs windows burst into bright light, and sound
spills out of the opening door, heavy beats of bass and drum, and
then a woman's voice kicks in, powerful and smooth like a marble
fist to the mouth. Eurythmics. *You have no FUCKING idea what
you've done.* Knox is speaking somewhere behind her, but she's ignoring him. Her motorcycle jacket is back on her body, her kilt
is reassembling itself around her hips, and she's gathering herself
together as she walks across the slick blacktop, stopping at the
unruly edge of the lawn. Severin remembers the rule. She pulls the
flier out of her pocket. The house is exactly as it was drawn, gables
and all. Behind it, the evergreens of Sehome stand silent and high.

The front door opens, and a man steps out. Severin holds up the
flier. He beckons to her, and she steps onto the court's soft lawn.

The lights wink out: the music stops.

For a brief, dizzying second, Severin thinks she's losing her balance—so complete and sudden is the lack of sound, it's as if the
entire planet shifted beneath her feet. She gasps and raises her
hands, anticipating the fall. It never comes.

This was a mistake: she turns, slow and deliberate, so as not to attract the inhabitants of the house, praying she'll see Knox. She'll fly across the street to him, silently admitting her mistake; and he'll fold her into his arms and whisk her away back to her ordinary little dorm, and all will be well.

She faces the now-darkened house.

Severin blinks, and turns.

She faces the house.

She made her choice, and the court holds her to it. She does not turn again.

Gradually, as though waking from a deep, antediluvian dream, the world blossoms back around her, above her, below. Stars studding the kodachromatic skies, winking and whispering their radio emissions across the velvet-green lands. The warm ocean of air, eddies and currents combing through the thick trees and caressing her face with its cedar-scented waves as it flows through the clearing. Crickets, cicadas and frogs, their songs of loneliness and love rising and falling, rising and falling. Fireflies, sparking and humming like miniature Tesla coils. Severin slips her jacket off, and it slithers to the grass in a series of thick whispers. Somewhere behind her in the world she can no longer see, in the suburban peaks and valleys of Bellingham, cold high autumn reigns. It is high summer here, so warm she tastes the perfume of ripening petals against her tongue. Severin bends down and stares at her boots, then steps out of them as they peel away from her flesh, leaving them beside her jacket. Then she does the same with her top, burning it away from her body with a single thought and letting the ashes float to the grass; and then her kilt slides off her hips. It looks as if some nameless girl was ripped out of her clothing, leaving it behind in a jumble as she was spirited away into the dusk.

And the door is still open. Here, in the legerdemain dark of the world, her magicked eyesight adjusts and the house reappears under scudding silver clouds and the ivory mass of the moon. Inside, nude shapes collide like columns of candle smoke and drift apart. Severin run a hand across her forehead, down her throat: it rests against the soft mound of her left breast, as if she is both cradling and caressing herself. The fireflies dart through the door, whirl and circle, gather close. The light grows bright and hard, begins moving forward. Severin wants to step back, but she's at the edge of the lawn—stepping back will only put her back at the edge of the lawn. This is what she wanted, anyway.

The light moves closer, of its own accord, seemingly—an old-fashioned lantern of glass and strawberry-red copper, polished to perfection, a slender round cage in which the fireflies swarm around and around in languid circles. It's only until it's a few feet out of the door and past the two low stone steps that Severin sees what's holding the round handle. A branch, dark and slender, devoid of needles or leaves. The lamp moves across the lawn, and the branch shows no sign of ending. It exudes from the doorway like placid water, smooth and graceful, its smaller limbs wrapped around the handle. Severin looks past the door, but sees no being, no creature at the branch's end. The flier is still in her hand, crumpled and damp. She lets it drift to the ground.

The lantern stops at the end of a small path of stones set into the grass. Severin stands, hesitant, waiting. As if from a far distance, she hears snatches and threads of familiar music, the soft throb of bass. The party is still happening, she realizes, back in the human world, as if it were simply around a corner and yet down a corridor that stretched for a million miles. Another branch splits from the main column, stretching out from underneath the lantern toward her. Knox's magic is still simmering inside her, and she reaches out her hand. Little bolts of pale red fire ripple down through her bones, push out and off her fingertips into the air as they touch the tips of the branch. It spirals around her fingers, slides away, runs a hard tip up the length of her pale white skin, resting in the veined crook of her arm before continuing up to her shoulder, then over and settling around one red nipple, curling itself in place.

Severin holds her breath. The branch pulses briefly, and a soft vibration spreads through the hardening tip, as though an invisible

tongue was tugging at the rapidly swelling skin. A wave of pleasure
rockets through her, so overwhelming that her knees buckle and
she pitches forward, grabbing the branch for support. She falls to
her knees on the soft grass, and lowers, letting the supple blades
brush up between her legs, sliding along her wet sex. Small sparks
collide and soar off her body in tiny arcs—Knox's magic, swelling
up out of her, too much for her to contain. He would know what
to do, if he were here. He would know how to take it back, how
to fly and soar with her through the placid streets of the town
until they crashed together in some secret quiet alley, turning her
inside-out as she burned in his grasp, coming in wave after wave as
his power flowed back out of her, until there was nothing left except her broken and satiated body in his arms, staring up through
the telephone wires at the cool grey beginning of day.

The thought of Knox sends Severin's hand darting out, as if to
grab and lower the branch from her breast to between her legs. But
once it detaches from her nipple, the wooden limb slips back and
away, and the lantern begins a slow retreat back toward the house.
Severin rises to her feet, brushing bits of dew-soaked grass from
her knees. Now the second branch is beckoning, its spindling ends
curling up over and over as if to say, *this way, child.* She follows,
stepping carefully onto each smooth flat stone as they draw nearer
to the house. The music is more than a suggestion now, but still
indistinguishable; and the light no greater. But Knox's magic has
combined with her lust, and the full power and extent of it courses
through her blood and sings out in her bones. The night is a ka-
leidoscope of endless variations of black, each more brilliant and
wondrous than the last, and she sees them all, she passes through
them and leaves infinite variations of her image in her wake, a
corridor of Severins that melt and drift upward into the trees and
catch on the wings of sleeping ravens and crows.

The lantern is inside the house now, and Severin follows, up the
stone steps and past the mundane summer screen door. Layers of
rooms on rooms, hallways and stairs and closets that open into

infinite realms; and people. As she passes them, following the lantern through its circuit of the house, she sees how they move back and forth between the other world and this one. Sloe-eyed men and women with scarecrow manes of hair and black lips, spiked dog collars at their necks and silver chains sliding around their rotating hips as they roll their lithe bodies back and forth in time; and then they are naked and glistening with the sheen of sex and earth, limbs wrapped around thick-furred creatures with amber eyes and antlers that slide between their lovers' legs, only the thick gasps and groans of their pleasure breaking the silence. Severin watches them all as she passes, watches tongues and lips lapping at crimson and purple folds of flesh, watches nimble hands guide hard, dark cocks as thick as young tree trunks deep inside quivering, eager mounds of flesh. They do not stop as she passes these rooms, but as she lingers in doorways, or along halls, hands reach out and caress her, heads bow down and lick her nipples, or rise up and nuzzle the cleft of her ass. Tongues dart out, sliding between her lips, hands grab hers and lower them into darkness, into hot wet orifices and around shuddering phalluses, slick with the fluids of others.

Someone hands her a cup—in one reality, it is a simple red plastic cup of beer, but here Severin raises a carved wooden bowl studded with strange flashing jewels to her lips, and wild honey pours into her mouth, honey that is not honey, that is something more, that sends her body into an enervated state of alertness. Everything, she sees everything in all its vast minute complexity now, the great woods beyond the walls of the house that whisper and sway and draw up power through the earth and spend it in showers over the land; the tiny goggles on the fireflies as they hover over the pools and piles of entwined limbs; the atonal echoings of extraterrestrial winds that blow through the subterranean chambers and rooms of the house; the beating of every heart, of every wing. Something large stops her, bends down and laps at the beads of honey trailing down her breasts. Severin reaches out, expecting horns. Only soft fur, wide ears, and the sensation of sharp fangs against her skin, a long rough tongue snaking out and down between her legs. Severin's head rolls back in ecstasy: she stares up at the ceiling, noting how she can see though it as if it were made of glass. Pine needles everywhere above her, green and brown like a cloak, and the sharp scent of pitch and musk in the air.

But the lantern is again beckoning her, its light bright and enticing; and she pushes the creature and his lovely tongue away and continues down the vast hallway, across rooms as wide as the campus, vaults as vast as the bay, through chambers as small and intimate as cradles. All of them filled with people, young men and women who look like her, or used to, trembling in the throes of numinous transformation. But is she not here at the command of the king? and is he not commanding her elsewhere? The honey's buzz has faded, and so has the light of the lantern, as it slips out what looks like an ordinary back door. Severin follows, stepping over supine bodies and back onto thick grass. And now the sensual cacophony of the house fades, and a profound and reverent peacefulness flows over her. The light of the lantern fades altogether, and she is standing in a sea of human men and women, all on their knees, heads down, hands out. They are bowing, she realizes, all in the same direction. They are genuflecting. They are worshipping.

Severin picks her way around the bodies. The ground is warm, free of twigs or rocks, and it feels like silk beneath her feet. All the bodies together form a wheel, she realizes as she makes her way in, a great wheel with thousands of spokes, radiating out from a center filled by the tallest, widest redwood she has ever seen in her life. She stops, stares up, up, up; and has to look away, vertigo washing over her. She sees the great trunk, the mass of branches like the clouds of a thunderstorm gathering overhead, she sees its end and yet it has no end; and when she concentrates on the land beneath her feet, Severin can feel that the redwood has no end in both directions, that it is everywhere, so painfully aware and alive that her mind reels in both joy and horror. This entire planet is an insect, it is nothing, and it is all held together by a being that dwarfs and transcends all of creation. In other universes, on other worlds, specks of life like her are making their way toward the tree, giving themselves over fully to the thought of their coming vastation. Letting out a small, ragged sigh, she continues on, weaving her way back and forth until she is standing several feet from the base of the tree in a small space in the sea of naked bodies that would exactly fit a young woman who has fallen to her knees.

And so she does, carefully planting her lower legs in the soft earth, moving her torso down until her breasts and face nestle against the ground, arms flung out in straight ley lines on either side of her head. And she waits.

The rise and fall of bodies, breathing. Somewhere, soft sobs. The warm night wind. Her buttocks are high in the air, legs slightly apart, nipples brushing the dirt. The wind flows around her limbs, caressing and cooling them even as it teases the warmth from her skin. She feels Knox's magic growling around inside her body like a trapped animal, once again waking up and seeking release. The ground shudders, little quakes sending cracks and rivulets of moving earth all around and under her. Another wave of desire floods her body, and she spreads her legs further apart, pressing and rubbing the tips of her breasts in slow circles until they grow hard again. Slowly and surely, that familiar sensation returns: the tugging at her nipples, as though hard lips were suckling at them. Severin's hips buck slightly—she presses down, then raises herself just enough to see. Yes, the branches, cresting the surface and clamped against her breasts, throbbing as they work their way around her tender flesh. A low moan escapes her lips, and all around her she hears the moans and sighs of the others, like a long wave gathering strength as it makes its way to the shore.

The redwood shudders. It's the sound of thunder, rolling down through the mountains and covering everything in its path in a surge of electric awe. Everyone grows still: Severin catches the breath in her throat and doesn't let it out. Beside her feet, she feels something burrowing its way to the surface, pushing the earth aside as it breaks free. Raising her head slightly, she looks between her breasts. A branch the size of a small tree trunk, bursting out of the earth. "No," she mutters, but it's too late—small whip-like branches erupt up and twine themselves around her wrists, while others wrap themselves again and again around her ankles, holding her fast. She pushes up; and the vines tighten, causing tears to squirt from her eyes at the pain. But the redwood is radiating red-hot desire now, and the magic in her blood responds, overriding her fear. Severin relaxes against the restraints, closing her eyes.

In the dark, in the clearing of the great forest, in the great wheel of humanity, Severin hears the eruption of something soft and wet. A quick, small touch against her naked inner thigh, followed by a longer caress, the gentle lappings of multiple tongues radiating from the soft velvet petals of a flower. Severin relaxes and tenses all at-once. The tongues work their way up the thick curve of her flesh, around the lower edge of her buttock, and then settle in between her legs. All around her, cries and groans; and her voice joins them. The entire mouth clamps itself firm between her legs as the tongues work their way around her flesh, sliding through every hot slick fold, roiling around the hard button of her clit, parting her like soft sand. Now she feels the hard round tip of something infinitely larger moving up through all the tongues, unsheathing itself from the branch and pressing its way in. Severin grunts and raises herself higher, and the branch responds, eagerly thrusting its way inside in a series of short, hard bursts. The ground is quaking hard now, and all around her she hears the shouting and howling of people in both pleasure and pain. She's so close now, the branch is moving in and out of her with lightning speed, and Severin can feel Knox's magic coalescing, coming together, expanding like magma—

She cries out as she comes, fireworks of pleasure bursting from her cunt and radiating all up and down her body—she cries out and she screams, as the magic drains away, sucked into the branch's proboscis, the voracious mouth of the redwood. Knox, bleeding away, her memories bleeding away, and the stars are fading and the screams and her own heartbeat and the wind rushing backwards into the night, and the flow and push of millions of others against her, the darkness and the explosions of pain and light; and upward, up and up, Severin and her million new eyes, her million new limbs, filtering up through all of the branches of the ages, and now there are stars too many stars to count and she is bursting up over them in an orgasmic shower of cosmic seed and dust that has no beginning or end and she is without beginning or end and then she is nothing at all, until it begins again, somewhere, someday, in some other universe, in some other part of her eternal king.

***

Knox stares out of Severin's dorm room window, four stories up, with its view of Sehome Forest and the great mountains beyond. He sees all across the curving folds of the land, from the highest upthrust of mountain to the most secret of crevices, to the thick shafts of wood springing from the moist land, bristling with seeded pine cones and dusty green needles. In this part of the wide world, he muses, humans raze the land, split the wood, and erect their houses, but they have no true home. They have no purchase. Here, it is the trees that weather the inland and ocean storms, that carry the white weight of pyroclastic flow with stoic grace; and when the winds blow, they do not break. They bend, ever so slightly, then snap back in a thunderous rush, thrusting back at the air even as they open their branches, letting brown seed scatter wide. This is the land of King Cupressaceae, and here he is all: Alpha and Omega, cock and cunt, the beginning and the end.

But this isn't his city, or planet, so what does he care?

"What the hell!"

A light flicks on, and Knox turns. Severin's roommate, the pretty, nervous girl whose energy tastes so fearfully sweet. She's sitting up in her bed, sheets chastely pulled up against her neck. As if he'd even entertain the thought.

"Oh, it's you. You scared me, I thought—what are you doing here? Where's Severin?"

Knox walks over to Severin's desk, and takes a small wooden box from the top shelf. "Severin and I—we broke up. She's not coming back."

"What? I don't understand. She's dropping out of school?"

Knox smiles. "You could say that." He starts for the door.

"Wait a minute! That's hers—you can't just take it!"

Knox turns. The girl hunches over, radiating fear. He lifts off, floats through the air like cigarette smoke toward the window.

"How do you do that?" she whispers. "Why did you teach Severin, and not me?"

"Because you're ordinary," Knox says as he slides through the cold glass, ignoring her piercing scream. "That's why you'll never know."

IT FEELS BETTER BITING DOWN

"What's with the lawnmower? No one mows this early in spring."

"It's June," I reply. "Spring should be long gone."

My twin sister rolls over onto her back, rubbing the afternoon sleep from her eyes with ten long pale fingers and two long pale thumbs. I'm lying next to her in our nest of pillows on the living room carpet, holding a book with hands that look just like hers, pale and strange, the extra finger curving into each palm, shy-like but not vestigial or immobile, not completely reticent. A sleeping stinger waiting to strike, my mother once said, in her raspy, rye-tinged voice. We like that.

"Where is it coming from?"

"Neighbors," I say. "Behind us. Not the sides."

"I didn't know someone new moved in." Sister sits up. That's what I call her anymore, and what she calls me. It drives our parents crazy, because we only answer to Sister, and they never know which one they're going to get when they call our name. It only started last summer, just before our senior year, but sometimes now I can't even remember our original names. We are Sister, a singular entity with twenty long fingers at the ends of our four pale hands.

"I know." I close the book and stare through the open-screened windows. Only the neighbor's roof is visible, framed by wind-tossed trees swaying under a cream blue sky. "No one's lived there for years. Remember Father complaining?"

"A white trash eyesore, he said."

"Property rates dropping, he said."

"All the plants dying," Sister says.

"Too many pine needles, too little sun," I say. "That whole back-yard is dead. The last owners graveled it over like a parking lot."

"What are they mowing then?" Sister asks.

The engine sputters and buzzes in a low, monotonous drone. The air pooling in through the open-screened windows smells of cut grass and gasoline. It smells enticing and new.

Sister stares at me, waiting for my response. I let the book slip from my hands. Mystery is blossoming behind the fence, waiting to be bit into like a stolen plum. We bare our teeth like wolves. We call it the delicious smile, because something strange and de-licious is about to be found, to be torn apart and sucked dry. It's another little thing that drives our parents insane, because it doesn't look anything like a smile at all.

I'm always the first to move. My sister likes to hang back a bit. I stand up and hold out my hand, and she reaches. I pull her to her feet with little effort on my part, our extra pinky fingers locked as she moves up toward me, a graceful pantomime of our violent birth. We make our way to through the silent house, hand in hand. Our parents are gone for the weekend—visiting friends, they said. They're probably just hiding out in a local motel. Sum-mers are hard for them because school is out and we're always around. To be fair, we don't make it easy. We never have, not since our unexpected birth. We're not stupid; we know how they feel about us. We see them as one with two sets of eyes. They don't like our indecipherable games, our private whisperings in secret languages, our twisty extra fingers brushing across their normal non-twisty things. Sometimes I feel bad. Only sometimes. They only ever wanted one of us to begin with, and anyway, this is what twins are. Wrong. This is how we're supposed to be.

By the time we get to the den and open the patio door, the mowing has stopped. A high-pitched fluting noise floods the air—it's the wind washing through all the construction sites surrounding our block, playing with chain link fences, weaving through empty, honeycombed frames of houses and apartment buildings, and stiff forests of construction beams half-driven into the hard ground. The skeletal remains of what was to be a new neighborhood, abandoned to ruin almost as quickly as it had begun. As we step outside, I raise my hands. I feel the warmth of the day, growing steady behind the cool gusts. In this part of the world it usually takes so long to throw off the winter cold, but this summer already feels different. We stand on the concrete slabs, looking across the yard at the fence. Father put it up a decade ago, when all the hedges started to wither and die off. In the slight gaps between each wide wooden slat, there's no movement or sound. We wait.

"Nobody's there," I finally whisper. "Maybe it was next door after all."

"I heard it, too."

"It's cold out. Let's go back inside."

Sister grabs a plastic lawn chair, and walks across the grass. Irritated, I stand at the patio's edge, toes curled over it and brushing the green blades as I watch. She places the lawn chair against the fence, then steps onto the fabric seat, pressing her face against the slats. Slowly she stands until her head peers over the top of the fence. Almost instantly, she crouches down, shock lighting up her face like the sun.

Come over here! she mouths, her hand beckoning. *There's a woman in the yard!*

I casually pick up a chair, dragging it through the grass as if this was the most boring thing in the world. Of course I want to see,

I wouldn't dream of not seeing, when Sister already has. I plunk the chair beside hers, and she shushes me, one long finger at her lips like she's our mother. Like she came first. It's times like this I want to grab her little fingers, snap them off her hands like beans from a vine.

What's wrong with you, she whispers as I step onto the chair.

What's wrong with you, I reply.

There's a woman, she's just standing there.

So what? Did you see a lawnmower?

No. Her face is all— Sister grimaces.

Is all what? I ask.

I can't describe it. You've just got to see.

I don't want her to see us.

She can't, Sister says. *Believe me.*

I hold out my hand. She clasps it, our stinger fingers coming together like a hook and eye. And just like that we're in sync again, we're Sister. In unison, we peer through the slats.

Behind the fence, a dark brown ranch house sits in the shade of several massive evergreens, their branches brushing the shingled roof. The surrounding yard is a carpet of pale gray gravel. No bushes or flowers, no potted plants or garden or fruit trees. A woman stands in the center of the yard, barefoot and wearing a shapeless green dress. The hem flutters in the wind, and her crooked brown hair floats about her shoulders, but she's as still as the house. She faces the fence. She faces us.

I let out a small gasp.

I know, Sister replies.

Together, we stand up until we're both staring over the top of the fence, our free hands clutching the rough wood for balance. The woman's face is like a statue, with only smooth, flesh-colored indentations where her eyes should be. The nose is small, and without nostrils—almost an afterthought. She has no eyebrows. Her mouth is her largest feature, wide with thin, sloppily painted purple lips that stretch across her cheeks almost to her small ears.

Relief floods my chest, and I turn to Sister.

"It's a mannequin," I say in a normal voice.

"It's a joke," she says, equally relieved.

"A lipstick smile," I say.

"An ugly wig," Sister says.

"What are you doing?" I ask. Sister slips from my grasp, and jumps down to the lawn. She bends down close to the edge of the fence, then holds up a small rock, the malicious smile on her face as she steps back onto the chair.

"I want to see her without it."

"Don't," I say.

"Why not?" she says.

"I don't know." I stare at the mannequin. "I don't think we should."

"It's just a mannequin."

"What if it's not?"

"What's gotten into you?"

"What's gotten into you?" We stare at each other, our frustration mutual.

"I don't want to fall." Sister reaches out. I grab her hand, but there's no enthusiasm in my touch. Sister pitches her right arm back, and throws the rock. We always did have good aim. It bounces with a plink right against the woman's forehead, and lands at her feet. After a second, the wig slithers to the woman's shoulders, exposing her marble round head.

I turn to Sister and smile. "Nice."

Sister smiles. "Nice."

"Niiiiiiicccccceeeeeeee." The woman's mouth is open, and the word is pouring out, elongated in the familiar lawnmower drone, in the thick smell of gasoline and severed green grass and torn leaves. We scream. Sister pushes back from the fence, her chair tipping over, but I don't let go of her hand. She falls against me, trying to pull away, but I throw my free arm over the top of the fence. I refuse to let go. The woman's lips stretch apart, wider than wide, past the nubby ears and up and up, until her entire face disappears in the bear trap of her mouth. It comes to a stop only when her entire head is split in half, the oval crown of her bald head resting at the back of her neck. Small rows of jagged teeth line the mouth's wet edges, rotating around and around like the blades of a circular saw.

"You wanted to be first," I say, to neither of us, to both of us. "You wanted to see."

"Let me go!" screams Sister. She pushes against me, but I'm wrapped tight against the fence, my feet hooked under the arms of the chair.

"No." I clench my hand tighter around hers, and I feel our bones grind and shift. The lawnmower sound deepens, grows ragged and clogged as if the blades were running over rocks. Small emerald specks are rising out of the woman's cavernous mouth, swarming about her head in a frothy cloud of bodies and wings. The smell is suffocating, and my body grows sleepy and numb. Sister feels like a thousand pounds of dead weight at my waist, but I can't push her off. It's not that we don't want to move any-more. It's that we can't. And then: an explosion of green pours out of the mouth, thousands of jewel-bright, stinging bodies that shoot forward, slam against the wood slats, against my face in a hard rain. The woman's body deflates, collapsing against the gravel in a shivering heap. I feel myself falling, finally. The sky is above me now, and the impossibly high tips of the trees, and Sister is somewhere beside me, grabbing at me with both hands. Everything grows hazy and beautiful and kitten-gray, even the screams. My right hand rests on my stomach, five fingers and one thumb clutching two objects, slender and soft and hard.

One of us is licking their lips and laughing. I'm pretty sure it's me.

***

Sister is crying. The mimicry tears, we call them. It's the kind of crying we do when we don't really want to cry but we have to, because everyone else is acting a certain way and we need to do the same. Her weeping sounds so far away and hollow, like she's become one of those empty construction lots, the wind plucking her bones like the metal frames, and threading the music back and forth across all the blocks.

My nose tickles. I think of tiny legs and wings, crawling out of my nostrils. I sit up, eyes open, and rub at my face until the sensation is gone. Then I stare down at my hands. Ten fingers, two thumbs. Two more fingers sit in my lap. I pick them up. The nails are polished and shiny, with a faint rose sheen. The other ends are perfectly round. No torn flesh, no peek of bones, no blood. I have a terrible urge to lick them. I manage to tuck one in the waistband of my pants before she speaks.

"What did you do to me?"

I look up. Sister is standing before me, her arms outstretched. Each hand has four perfect fingers, and one pretty little thumb. I hold up her extra pinky.

"I only have the one."

"Well, where is the other?"

"I can't keep track of your fingers for you."

"I look all normal now."

"Yes, like that's *so* horrible."

"It is!"

"I know how you really feel."

Sister looks frightened, but she stops pretending to cry. I roll my eyes, and turn back to the fence. Between the slats, I catch glimpses of flesh, folds of grayish white dotted with emerald specks, and the shimmer of sharp teeth catching the midday sun. A thin breeze pushes through the fence. It smells like rotting fruit, sour-sweet.

"That was not a mannequin," I say.

"Give me my finger back."

"What were those flying things?"

"It doesn't matter," Sister says.

"I think it matters quite a lot," I say, standing up. "Show me your hands again."

Sister holds them out. I place the end of the pinky next to the red bump where it used to hang. "It's like it just fell off," she says. "It doesn't even hurt."

"You're relieved, aren't you."

"I don't know how I feel."

"We're not the same anymore," I say. "We're not the same person."

"Is that all you care about?" she says. "We never were."

I place her pinky next to mine, touching the end to my skin. A sharp pain spikes through my hands, and my left extra pinky trembles, then unfurls. It isn't curled up in sleep anymore. It's strong and straight, and the nail is long and steel-sharp. I wiggle it back and forth. I've never been able to do that before. We stand on the lawn in silence, staring at it. Across the fence, crows are gathering on the rooftops, waiting for the right moment to attack the woman's remains. I press Sister's pinky hard against my skin, taking my hand away only when the ache subsides. It doesn't fall off.

"What did you do?"

I wiggle the fingers on my left hand. All six of them, and a thumb.

"That was my finger!" Sister steps forward, but I step forward, too, my sharp-nailed finger extended. She pulls back.

"Finders, keepers." I reach down into my waistband and pull out her other finger. "Losers, weepers."

Sister lunges. I open my mouth wide. A soft, low metallic buzz emerges from the back of my throat, and the drowsy scent of gasoline fills the air. Sister's pupils widen, and her body grows slack. "Two can play, Sister," she murmurs, and sticks out her emerald-flecked tongue. My knees buckle at the scent—fresh-cut grass and crushed leaves, all the ripe green distress of dying flora. I sigh, and my breath commingles with hers. We drop to our knees.

"Give me my fingers back!"

"They're our fingers."

"We're not the same."

"Not yet." I make the words rattle like a saw.

Sister grabs my hand and puts my index finger in her mouth. I slap her face, and when she raise her other hand, I grab it, and catch her wriggling thumb with my teeth. We fall against the fence, and slide sideways onto the ground, our noses almost touching.

"You're only hurting yourself." Her hot tongue pushes the words around my flesh.

"You love it."

She smiles the delicious smile.

We both bite down.

Behind the fence, the crows have landed, fighting over the woman's festering remains. Sister lies on the grass with her head at my shoulder, examining my severed finger. It didn't even hurt a bit. And her thumb—it was like nipping off cookie dough from the roll. Other than several small teeth marks that quickly faded away, you couldn't tell what was gone. She's placed it in the middle of her palm, and now it waves back and forth, around and around. I take her thumb, and place it between my breasts, then slide it down to the open zipper of my pants.

"Absolutely not," Sister says.

"Absolutely yes," I say.

"That's disgusting."

"It's practical. It leaves my hands free for the other things."

"I can't believe you just said that."

I roll over so that our noses are touching again, our foreheads, our lips. "If you don't like what I'm saying, then why don't you bite off my tongue."

She does. In our petroleum haze, we shed our clothes, adjusting and arranging our new parts. Insects float in and out of our now-empty mouths, catch in our long hair, crown our heads like emerald halos. Sister signals me, her long fingers waving me forward,

and we move as one across the sun-dappled yard to a far corner,
to a bed of beauty bark under the heavy needled branches of stiff
evergreens. The afternoon sun lowers and the moon rises, bright
and clear in the hot summer night. Our limbs come together, fall
apart and weave together again, tongues and toes and scent directing our exploration. And with the break of day, we grow bold with
our new single mouth, and bite down harder, further within, until
we are inside-out, until our hearts are one. Black birds gather on
the overhead branches, chattering at the sight of so many organs,
so much sinew and broken bone. They wait in vain. We are fast
and quick and sure, and not a drop of blood is spilled or misspent.

And night falls again. We rise from our corner, stretch our dou-
ble-length torso and our many slender double-jointed limbs, raise
the eyes of our single-mouthed head to a star-studded sky as we
step into the center of the lawn. The wind is low, and the birds
are quiet. All about us, small backyards pool behind hedges and
fences, small oases of suburban repose. And across the concrete patio, yellow light wells from the kitchen window, and two familiar
figures move like shadow puppets in a box. With two sets of eyes,
we watch as one.

"Sister," I say.

"Our parents are home," I say.

"Do we show them?" I ask. "Do we embrace them?"

"How can we not?" I say.

"They will scream," I say.

"And then they will love it," I say.

"Or they will die," I say.

"Unless we die, as the woman did," I say.

"She gave us a gift," I say.

"And where is she now," I say.

We grow silent.

After a time, we lower our haunches onto the dew-speckled
grass. One long multi-fingered arm picks up a sandal, discarded
from two days ago. It seems so small. Our parents move back and

forth deep within the house, talking, drinking, making dinner. They look happy. We think of the woman, immobile in a barren landscape, staring with empty eyes past our fence, dreaming of the lush, forbidden world of another backyard.

ALLOCHTHON

North Bonneville, 1934

Ruth sits in the kitchen of her company-built house, slowly turning the pages of her scrapbook. The clock on the
bookcase chimes ten. In the next room, the only other
room, she hears her husband getting dressed. He's deliberately slow
on Sundays, but he's earned the right. Something about work, he's
saying from behind the door. Something about the men. Ruth
can't be bothered to listen. She stares at the torn magazine clipping
taped to a page. It's a photo of an East Coast socialite vacation-
ing somewhere in the southern tropics: a pretty young woman in
immaculate white linens, lounging on a bench that encircles the
impossibly thick trunk of a palm tree. All around the woman and
the tree, a soft manicured lawn flows like a velvet sea, and the skies
above are clear and dry. Ruth runs her free hand across the back of
her neck, imagining the heat in the photo, the lovely bite and sear
of an unfiltered sun. Her gaze wanders up to the ceiling. Not even
a year old, and already rain and mold have seeped through the
shingled roof, staining the cream surface with hideous blossoms.
It's supposed to be summer, yet always the overcast skies in this
part of the country, always the clouds and the rain. She turns the
page. More photos and ephemera, all the things that over the years
have caught her eye. But all she sees is the massive palm, lush and

hard and tall, the woman's back curved into it like a drowsy lover, the empty space around them, above and below, as if they are the only objects that have ever existed in the history of time.

Henry walks into the room and grabs his coat, motioning for her to do the same. Ruth clenches her jaw and closes the scrapbook. Once again, she's made a promise she doesn't want to keep. But she doesn't care enough to speak her mind, and, anyway, it's time to go.

Their next-door neighbor steers his rusting car down the dirt road, past the edges of the town and onto the makeshift highway. His car is one of many, a caravan of beat-up trucks and buggies and jalopies. Ruth sits in the back seat with a basket of rolls on her lap, next to the other wife. It started earlier in the week as an informal suggestion over a session of grocery shopping and gossip by some of the women, and now almost forty people are going. A weekend escape from the routine of their dreary lives to a small park further down the Columbia River, far from the massive construction site for the largest dam in the world, which within the decade will throttle the river's power into useful submission. The wives will set up the picnic, a potluck of whatever they can afford to offer, while they gossip and look after the children. The men will eat and drink, complain about their women and their jobs and the general rotten state of affairs across the land, and then they'll climb a trail over eight hundred feet high, to the top of an ancient volcanic core known as Beacon Rock.

The company wife speaks in an endless paragraph, animate and excited. Billie or Betty or Becky, some childish, interchangeable name. She's four months pregnant and endlessly, vocally grateful that her husband found work on a WPA project when so many in the country are doing without. Something about the Depression. Something about the town. Something about schools. Ruth can't be bothered. She bares her teeth, nods her head, makes those ridiculous clucking sounds like the other wives would, all those bitches with airs. Two hours of this pass, the unnatural rattle and groan of the engines, the monotonous roll of pine-covered hills. The image of the palm tree has fled her mind. It's only her on the lawn, alone, under the unhinged jaw of the sky. Something about dresses. Something about the picnic. Something about a cave—

Ruth snaps to attention. There is a map in her hands, a crude drawing of what looks like a jagged-topped egg covered in zigzagging lines. This is the trail the men are going to take, the wife is explaining. Over fifty switchbacks. A labyrinth, a maze. The caravan has stopped. Ruth rubs her eyes. She's used to this, these hitches of lost time. Monotonous life, gloriously washed away in the backwater tides of her waking dreams. She stumbles out of the car, swaying as she clutches the door. The world has been reduced to an iron-gray bowl of silence and vertigo, contained yet infinite. Mountains and space and sky, all around, with the river diminished to a soft mosquito's whine. Nausea swells at the back of her throat, and a faint, pain-tinged ringing floods her ears. She feels drunk, unmoored. Somewhere, Henry is telling her to turn, to look. There it is, he's saying, as he tugs her sleeve like a child. Ruth spirals around, her tearing eyes searching, searching the horizon, until finally she—

Something about—

***

—the rock.

Ruth lifts her head. She's sitting at her kitchen table, a cup of lukewarm coffee at her hand. The scrapbook is before her, open, expectant, and her other hand has a page raised, halfway through the turn. On the right side of the book, the woman in the southern tropics reclines at her palm in the endless grass sea, waiting.

Henry stands before her, hat on head, speaking. —Ruthie, quit yer dreamin' and get your coat on. Time to go.

—Go where.

—Like we planned. To Beacon Rock.

The clock on the bookcase chimes ten.

Outside, a plane flies overhead, the sonorous engine drone rising and falling as it passes. Ruth rubs her eyes, concentrating. Every day in this colorless town at the edge of this colorless land is like the one before, indistinguishable and unchanging. She doesn't remember waking up, getting dressed, making coffee. And there's something outside, a presence, an all-consuming black static wave of sound, building up just beyond the wall of morning's silence, behind the plane's mournful song. She furrows her brow, straining to hear.

Henry speaks, and the words sound like the low rumble of avalanching rock as they fall away from his face. It's language, but Ruth doesn't know what it means.

—Gimme a moment, I'm gonna be sick, Ruth says to no one in particular as she pushes away from the table. She doesn't bother to close the front door as she walks down the rickety step into warm air and a hard gray sun. Ruth stumbles around the house to the back, where she stops, placing both hands against the wooden walls as she bends down, breathing hard, willing the vomit to stay down. Gradually, the thick sticky feeling recedes, and the tiny spots of black that dance around the corners of her vision fade and disappear. She stands, and starts down the dusty alley between the rows of houses and shacks.

Mountains, slung low against the far horizon of the earth, shimmering green and gray in the clear quiet light. Ruth stops at the edge of the alley, licking her lips as she stands and stares. Her back aches. Beyond the wave and curve of land, there is… Ruth bends over again, then squats, cupping her head in her hands, elbows on knees. This day, this day already happened. She's certain of it. They drove, they drove along the dirt highway, the woman beside her, mouth running like a hurricane. They hung to the edges of the wide river, and then they rounded the last curve and stopped, and Ruth pooled out of the car like saliva around the heavy shaft of a cock, and she looked up, and, and, and.

And now some company brat is asking her if she's okay, hey lady are you sick or just taking a crap, giggling as he speaks. Ruth stands up, and slaps him, crisp and hard. The boy gasps, then disappears between the houses. Ruth clenches her jaw, trying not to cry as she heads back around the house. Henry stands beside the open car door, ruin and rage dancing over his face. Her coat and purse and the basket of rolls have been tossed in the back seat, next to the wife. She's already talking up a storm, rubbing her belly while she stares at Ruth's, her eyes and mouth all smug and smarmy in that oily sisterly way, as if she knows. As if she could know anything at all.

The sky above is molten lead, bank after bank of roiling dark clouds vomiting out of celestial foundries. Ruth cranks the window lever, presses her nose against the crack. The air smells vast and earthen. The low mountains flow past in frozen antediluvian waves. Something about casseroles, the company bitch says. Something about gelatin and babies. Something about low tides. Ruth touches her forehead, frowns. There's a hole in her memory, borderless and black, and she feels fragile and small. Not that she hates the feeling. Not entirely. Her hand rises up to the window's edge, fingers splayed wide, as if clawing the land aside to reveal its piston-shaped core. The distant horizon undulates against the dull light, against her flesh, but fails to yield. It's not its place to. She knows she's already been to Beacon Rock. Lost deep inside, a trace remains. She got out of the car and she turned, and the mountains and the evergreens and thrusting up from the middle, a geologic eruption, a disruption hard and wide and high and then: nothing. Something was there, some thing was there, she knows she saw it, but the sinkhole in her mind has swallowed all but the slippery edges.

Her mouth twists, silent, trying to form words that would describe what lies beyond that absence of sound and silence and darkness and light, outside and in her head. As if words like that could exist. And now they are there, the car is rounding the highway's final curves before the park. She rolls down the window all the way, and sticks her head and right arm out. A continent behind, her body is following her arm, like a larva wriggling and popping out of desiccated flesh, out of the car, away from the shouting, the ugly engine sounds, into the great shuddering static storm breaking all around. She saw Beacon Rock, then and now. The rest, they all saw the rock, but she saw beyond it, under the volcanic layers she saw it, and now she feels it, now she hears, and it hears her, too.

Falling, she looks up as she reaches out, and—

***

The clock on the bookcase chimes ten. Her fingers, cramping, slowly uncurl from a cold coffee cup. Henry is in the other room, getting dressed. Ruth hears him speaking to her, his voice tired water dribbling over worn gravel. Something about the company picnic. Something about malformed, moldering backwaters of trapped space and geologic time. Something about the rock.

Tiny spattering sounds against paper make her stare up to the ceiling, then down at the table. Droplets of blood splash against the open page in her scrapbook. Ruth raises her hand to her nose, pinching the nostrils as she raises her face again. Blood slides against the back of her throat, and she swallows. On the clipping, the young socialite's face disappears in a sudden crimson burst, like a miniature solar flare erupting around her head, enveloping her white-teethed smile. Red coronas everywhere, on her linen-draped limbs, on the thick bark of the palm, on the phosphorus-bright velvet lawn. Somewhere outside, a plane drones overhead, or so it sounds like a plane. No, a plain, a wide expanse of plain, a moorless prairie of static and sound, all the leftover birth and battle and death cries of the planet, jumbled into one relentless wave streaming forth from some lost and wayward protrusion at the earth's end. Ruth pushes the scrapbook away and wipes her drying nose with the edges of her cardigan and the backs of her hands. Her lips open and close in silence as she tries to visualize, to speak the words that would describe what it is that's out there, what waits for her, high as a mountain and cold and alone. What is it that breathes her name into the wind like a mindless burst of radio static, what pulses and booms against each rushing thrust of the wide river, drawing her body near and her mind away? She saw and she wants to see it again and she wants to remember, she wants to feel the ancient granite against her tongue, she wants to rub open-legged against it until it enters and hollows her out like a mindless pink shell. She wants to fall into it, and never return here again.

—Not again, she says to the ceiling, to the walls, as Henry opens the door. —Not again, not again, not again.

He stares at her briefly, noting the red flecks crusting her nostrils and upper lip. —Take care of that, he says; grabbing his coat, he motions at the kitchen sink. Always the same journey, and the destination never any closer. Ruth quickly washes her face, then slips out the door behind him into the hot, sunless morning. The company wife is in the back, patting the seat next to her. Something about the weather, she says, her mouth spitting out the words in little squirts of smirk while her eyes dart over Ruth's wet red face. She thinks she knows what that's all about. Lots of company wives walk into doors. Something about the end of Prohibition. Something about the ghosts of a long-ago war. Ruth sits with her head against the window, eyes closed, letting the one-sided conversation flow out of the woman like vomit. Her hand slips under the blue-checked dish towel covering the rolls, and she runs her fingers over the flour-dusted tops. Like cobblestones. River stones, soft water-licked pebbles, thick gravel crunching under her feet. She pushes a finger through the soft crust of a roll, digging down deep into its soft middle. That's what it's doing to her, out there, punching through her head and thrusting its basalt self all through her, pulverizing her organs and liquefying her heart. The car whines and rattles as it slams in and out of potholes, gears grinding as the company man navigates the curves. Eyes still shut, Ruth runs a fingertip over each lid, pressing in firm circles against the skin, feeling the hard jelly mounds roll back and forth at her touch until they ache. The landscape outside reforms itself as a negative against her lids, gnarled and blasted mountains rimmed in small explosions of sulfur-yellow light. She can see it, almost the tip of it, pulsating with a monstrous beauty in the distance, past the last high ridges of land. Someone else must have known, and that's why they named it so. A wild perversion of nature, calling out through the everlasting sepulcher of night, seeking out and casting its blind gaze only upon her—

The company wife is grabbing her arm. The car has stopped. Henry and the man are outside, fumbling with the smoking engine hood. Ruth wrests her arm away from the woman's touch, and opens the door. The rest of the caravan has passed them by, rounded the corner into the park. Ruth starts down the side of the road, slow, nonchalant, as if taking in a bit of air. As if she could. The air has bled out, and only the pounding static silence remains, filling her throat and lungs with its hadal-deep song. —I'm coming, she says to it. —I'm almost here. She hears the wife behind her, and picks up her pace.

—You gals don't wander too far, she hears the company man call out. —We should have this fixed in a jiffy.

Ruth kicks her shoes off and runs. Behind her, the woman is calling out to the men. Ruth drops her purse. She runs like she used to when she was a kid, a freckled tomboy racing through the wheat fields of her father's farm in North Dakota. She runs like an animal, and now the land and the trees and the banks of the river are moving fast, slipping past her piston legs along with the long bend of the road. Her lungs are on fire and her heart is all crazy and jumpy against her breasts and tears streak into her mouth and nose and it doesn't matter because she is so close and it's calling her with the hook of its song and pulling her reeling her in and

Henry's hand is at the back of her neck and there's gravel and the road smashing against her mouth and blood and she's grinding away and kicking and clawing forward and all she has to do is lift up her head just a little bit and keep her eyes shut and she will finally see—

***

Ruth's hands are clasped tight in her lap. Scum floats across the surface of an almost empty cup of coffee. A sob escapes her mouth, and she claps her hand over it, hitching as she pushes it back down. This small house. This small life. This cage. She can't do it anymore. The clock on the bookcase chimes ten. —I swear, this is the last time, Ruth says, wiping the tears from her cheeks. The room is empty, but she knows who she's speaking to. It knows, too. —I know how to git to you. I know how to see you. This is the last goddamn day.

On the kitchen table before her is the scrapbook, open to her favorite clipping. Ruth peels it carefully from the yellowing page and holds it up to the light. Somewhere in the southern tropics: a pretty young woman in stained white linens, lounging on a bench that encircles the impossibly thick trunk of a tree that has no beginning or end, whose roots plunge so far beyond the ends of earth and time that, somewhere in the vast cosmic oceans above, they loop and descend and transform into the thick fronds and leaves that crown the woman's head with dappled shadow. All around the woman and the tree, drops of dried blood are spattered across the paper like the tears of a dying sun. The woman's face lies behind one circle of deep brown, earth brown, wood brown, corpse brown. She is smiling, open-eyed, breathing it all in. Ruth balls the clipping up tight, then places it in her mouth, chewing just a bit before she swallows. There is no other place the woman and the palm have been, that they will ever be. Alone, apart, removed, untouched. All life here flows around them, utterly repelled. They cannot be bothered. It is of no concern to them. What cycle of life they are one with was not born in this universe.

In the other room, Henry is getting dressed. If he's talking, she can't hear. Everywhere, black static rushes through the air, strange equations and latitudes and lost languages and wondrous geometries crammed into a silence so old and deep that all other sounds are made void. Ruth closes the scrapbook and stands, wiping the sweat from her palms on her Sunday dress. There is a large knife in the kitchen drawer, and a small axe by the fireplace. She chooses the knife. She knows it better, she knows the heft of it in her hand when slicing into meat and bone. When he finally opens the door and steps into the small room, she's separating the rolls, the blade slipping back and forth through the powdery grooves. Ruth lifts one up to Henry, and he takes it. It barely touches his mouth before she stabs him in the stomach, just above the belt, where nothing hard can halt its descent. He collapses, and she falls with him, pulling the knife out and sitting on his chest as she plunges it into the center of his chest, twice because she isn't quite sure where his heart is, then once at the base of his throat. Blood, like water gurgling over river stones, trickling away to a distant, invisible sea. That, she can hear. Ruth wipes the blade on her dress as she rises, then places it on the table, picks up the basket and walks to the front door. She opens it a crack.

—Henry's real sick, she says to the company man. —We're gonna stay home today. She gives him the rolls, staring hard at the company wife in the back seat as he walks back to his car. The wife looks her over, confused. Ruth shuts the door. That bitch doesn't know a single thing.

Ruth slips out the back, through the window of their small bedroom. The caravan of cars is already headed toward the highway, following the Columbia downstream toward Beacon Rock. They'll never make it to their picnic. They'll never see it. They never do. She moves through the alley, past the last sad row of company houses and into the tall evergreens that mark the end of North

Bonneville. With each step into the forest, she feels the weight of the town fall away a little, and something vast and leviathan burrows deeper within, filling up the unoccupied space. When she's gone far and long enough that she no longer remembers her name, she stops, and presses her fingers deep into her sockets, scooping her eyes out and pinching off the long ropes of flesh that follow them out of her body like sticky yarn. What rushes from her mouth might be screaming or might be her soul, and it is smothered in the indifferent silence of the wild world.

And now it sees, and it moves in the way it sees, floating and darting back and forth through the hidden phosphorescent folds of the lands within the land, darkness punctured and coruscant with unnamable colors and light, its dying flesh creeping and hitching through forests petrified by the absence of time, past impenetrable ridges of mountains whose needle-sharp peaks cut whorls in the passing rivers of stars. A veil of flies hovers about the caves of its eyes and mouth, rising and falling with every rotting step, and bits of flesh scatter and sink to the earth like barren seeds next to its pomegranate blood. If there is pain, it is beyond such narrow acknowledgement of its body. There is only the bright beacon of light and thunderous song, the sonorous ringing of towering monolithic basalt breathing in and out, pushing the darkness away. There is, finally, past the curvature of the overgrown wild, a lush grass plain of emerald green, ripe and plump under a fat hot sun, a wide bench of polished wood, and a palm tree pressing in a perfect arc against its small back, warm and worn and hard like ancient stone. When it looks up, it cannot see the tree's end. Its vision rises blank and wondrous with branches as limitless as both their dreams, past all the edges of all time, and this is the way it should be.

FURNACE

E veryone knew our town was dying, long before we truly saw it. There's a certain way a piece of fruit begins to wrinkle and soften, caves in on itself around the edges of a fast-appearing bruise, throwing off the sickly-sweet scent of decay and death that always attracts some creeping hungry thing. Some part of the town, an unused building sinking into its foundations, a forgotten alleyway erupting into a slow maelstrom of weeds and cracked stone, was succumbing, had festered, had succumbed: and now threw off the warning spores of its demise. Everywhere in the town we went about the ins and outs of our daily lives and business, telling ourselves everything was normal, everything was fine. And every now and then a spore drifted into our lungs, riding in on a faint thread of that rotting fruiting scent, and though we did not pause in our daily routines, we stumbled a bit, we slowed. It was the last days of summer, I had just turned thirteen, and the leaves were beginning to turn, people were gathering the final crops of their fine little backyard gardens, culling the lingering remains of the season's foods and flowers, smoothing over the soil. My grandfather had placed a large red-rusted oil barrel off the side of the garage, and every evening he threw the gathering detritus of summer into the can, and set it on fire. Great plumes of black smoke rose into the warm air, feather-fine flakes of ash and hot red sparks. I stood on the gravel path, watching the bright red licks of fire crackle and leap from the barrel's jagged edges as my grandfather poked the burning sticks and leaves further down. An evening wind carried the dark smoke up into the canopy of branches overhead, tall evergreens swaying and whispering as they swept and sifted the ash further into the sky. We watched in silence. The air smelled gritty and smoky and dark, in that way the air only ever smells at the end of a dying summer, the smell of the sinking sun and dark approaching fall. The trees shifted, the branches changed direction, and the sickly-sweet scent caught in our throats, driving the smoke away.

—What is that? I asked.

—I don't know, my grandfather replied. He rubbed ash from his eyes, and stared out into a distance place neither of us could see. —Something's wrong.

***

Summer officially ended, school began, and the town continued. It was easy for all of us to say that everything was fine. The dissonance in the air was the usual changing of the seasons, we told ourselves. Near the downtown area, on a small lonely street along the outskirts of the factories and warehouses that ringed the downtown district, that strange and troubling area where suburbia fizzled out to its bitter end and the so-called city proper began, a number of small businesses closed with no warning to their loyal long-time customers or to those who worked for them. I knew of this only because my mother drove down that particular street one early afternoon, having taken me out of school for a dentist appointment. My mother had frequented most of these stores in her childhood, and she loved driving down the street as an adult, pointing out to me all the various places she had been taken by my grandfather. A small confectioner's store that supplied those queer square mint-tinged wafers that were both creamy and crunchy, the pastel sweets popular at weddings and wakes. A stationer's store, where my mother's family had bought boxes and boxes of thick cream paper and envelopes with the family crest, a horned griffin rampant over a field of night-blooming cereus, and where my grandfather bought business cards and memo pads with his name printed neatly in the middle, just above his title of supervisor for the town's electric and water company. A dilapidated movie theater that showed films in languages no one had ever heard of, from countries no one could ever seem to recall having seen on our schools' and library's aging maps and globes. A haberdashery where my father once had his soft brown wool felt fedoras and thick lambskin winter gloves blocked and stitched to his exact measurements and specifications. It had been taken over just that spring by the son of the former owner, an earnest and intense young man with perfect pale skin and unruly black hair, and unfortunately large black eyes. All three of those stores and more sat dark and fallow all along the block, faded red CLOSED and OUT OF BUSINESS signs swinging against padlocked doors, display windows choked with cobwebs and dust, the now familiar odor of sickly sweetness lingering in the air.

—Why do I keep smelling that, I said, pinching my nose shut. —What is it?

—It smells like camphor, my mother said.

—What's that?

—Like the mothballs in our closets, she said. —You know, what I use to keep your father's and grandmother's things from molding and rotting away. To preserve things.

—Preserve? Like jam?

—In a way. To protect things. So they'll never grow old, and always stay the same.

That afternoon as my mother steered the car along the narrow meridian dividing the street in two, the pale young man stood outside the haberdashery's doors, his long arms wrapped around a bolt of fabric as if he were carrying the body of a dead child. I started in shock to realize it was not a bolt of fabric, but a length of thick grey wool wrapped around the stiff body of a large bird with two beaks twisted into a hideous spiral and a spider-like cluster of lidless coal-colored eyes. My mother stopped the car, and we stepped onto the dry worn street sitting under a cool and cloudless sky crowned by telephone wires. No one else was here this time of the afternoon in this part of the town, a part of the town in the middle of everything yet nowhere in particular, where the buildings rose no more than two stories before flattening out in resignation and despair, where you could walk down the sidewalks for hours, see no strip mall or market or house that didn't look like the one behind it and before, hear only the soft crinkle of your shoes against cracked cement and the occasional miserable distant bark of a dog. In hindsight, we should have been more vigilant, more aware that these were the places of a town where septicemia and putrification creep in first, those lonely and familiar sections we slipped into and through every day without concern or care—not the seedy crumbling but flashy edges where decay was expected, and, from a certain element of our small society, even accepted and encouraged. These quiet streets of lonely backwater districts, these were the places we never gave a single thought about, because we thought they would be here forever, unchanging in the antiseptic amber of our fixed memories. These quiet streets of lonely backwater districts were always the first to go.

—Don't come any closer, said the pale young man to my mother as she stepped onto the sidewalk.

—What happened to all the stores? my mother asked. —When did everything close?

—Don't go near the windows, said the pale young man. — It's terrible, don't look. He stepped forward as if to block her, his already too large eyes widening further, the rims and lids as purple-red as the leaves on the trees, as if he had been weeping for hours, for centuries. My mother, a woman who, like her father, my grandfather, did not pay much heed to the general spoken and unspoken rules of a town, brushed past him, and I followed in her wake, already at thirteen very much a similar stubborn member of my family. My mother stepped up to one of the display windows, and I to the other, cupping my hands around my eyes to block out the sun as I pressed my face against the glass. —Don't look, the young man repeated, but he did nothing to stop us, only stood on the sidewalk cradling his many-eyed black-feathered bird wrapped in fabric, shivering in the afternoon sun. Inside the store, everything appeared covered in the light dust typical of such a place, but nothing appeared out of the ordinary. I had last been in the store five years ago, to help my mother pick out a fine linen handkerchief for my father for the holidays, before he had disappeared in the deep network of tunnels and passages owned by the town's electric and water company. I kept staring through the glass. Bowlers and fedoras slumping over the resigned foreheads of cracked mannequin heads, weary trays of uneven chevron-covered ties, unpolished cufflinks depressed into velvet folds of faded burgundy. My breath fogged the glass, and I wiped it away with a pass of my hands. Everything was quiet, peaceful, still.

—I don't see anything different, my mother said. —Everything looks the same as I remember. This is the way it should be.

—I know, the young man said. —It all looks the same on the outside. It always has. You have to look underneath.

—How can one look underneath? I asked.

—You just do. You just know.

I'm not certain how long we stood on the quiet sidewalk of the lonely street in that empty part of town, staring through finger-print-smeared windows into darkness. I now only remember how after a time had passed and as the afternoon sun hitched further down toward the town's jagged horizon, everything in the store seemed to recede, sink into an interminable black fuzz not un-like mold spreading across fruit. Soft sweet mold and mannequin heads, and no life at all in the displays and counters and fixtures and heavy folds of fabric, only the amber-tinged cool approaching dark. My eyes adjusted to the fading light, and everything in the haberdashery blurred and shifted into a single indistinct mass: for one wild terrible second I felt like I was staring into the only place left in the world, that there was only my face pressed to the glass front of a dead forgotten store endlessly out of the reach of my immovable limbs, and everything and everyone behind me, including myself, was forever gone.

—Nothing's changed except the sign, my mother said. —This is unacceptable. The stores must be reopened, so we can shop here, as we've always done. That's how it's supposed to be.

The young man replied, —Yes. And it will never end.

My mother looked at him, but did not reply.

I stepped back from the glass, and as I did, I caught a glimpse of the pale young man's face, reflected beneath the faded gold letters of the haberdashery that bore his father's name. I saw underneath him. I saw his wide unmoving mouth, his tiny painted teeth, his lidless lashless eyes, his cool matte porcelain skin. It was then I remembered I had crushed on him briefly, that last spring. I'd told my mother how handsome he looked, how comforting and familiar, and she'd laughed me into embarrassed silence, and so I'd driven it from my mind. The young man turned from us, and as he walked down the sidewalk back into suburbia, trailing oily iridescent feathers at his feet and the numbing sweet smell of camphor through the air, I caught a glimpse of his neck below his black, black hair, and the straight bloodless seam like a strange new road, slicing through every part of the town I'd ever known.

***

My mother drove us home in silence, and we never spoke of the incident to each other again. I believe I was afraid to ask my mother what she meant when she said she saw nothing underneath, whether she meant she saw nothing out of the ordinary, or if she meant that she had perceived that same black nothingness the pale young man claimed he saw welling beneath the surface of the haberdashery, the nothingness that had spread throughout that entire row of stores. I was afraid to ask my mother what she meant when she saw nothing underneath, nothing changed, and said that was the way it should always be. I believe I knew then what I was afraid of, or rather there was a confirmation within me of what I had always known that I was afraid of; and my mother knew that I knew, and together in silence we drove home.

We drove down the street several weeks later. All of the stores displayed their usual faded yet cheerful red and white OPEN signs, but my mother didn't slow the car, nor did she spin her usual tales of how her family had frequented the various shops over the years and what items she bought that were still somewhere in our house, carefully packed in cedar boxes lined with tissue paper and small white mothballs. I slid down in the car seat until my eyes were level with the plastic button lock on the door, and stared out the window at the haberdashery. Sitting on the sidewalk beside the dusty glass door, still holding the stiff deformed bird bundled in wool felt, I saw the pale young man that for one brief second in my past I had crushed on like the soles of my feet against soft gray gravel, standing, staring out into the street, the look on his face not unlike that of my grandfather when he stood over the can of burning leaves and ash. I had never told my mother what I thought I'd seen that strange afternoon in the face of the pale young man, or at the back of his neck. I didn't need to. My mother smiled, and stared ahead, and drove on.

Fall deepened and thickened and the air above and over our heads grew cold, but the gold and red leaves and the earth itself were still hot to the touch, as though the trees were drawing up and throwing off some unseen underground fire. I woke up early in the morning, having slept every night with the light at my desk never off and the small television always tuned to movies so old even my grandfather had never heard of them. I dressed for school to the snowy images of sleek, long-dead women and men, drifting through a world constructed solely of pixilated shades of black and grey. My grandfather seemed never to sleep, spending evenings after work in the kitchen, spreading maps and charts of the town's systems and infrastructures over the table, scribbling indecipherable equations and geometric shapes in blue ball-point pen across the outlines of our streets and neighborhoods he'd traced onto wide sheets of translucent onionskin, the low light of the kitchen lamp falling over his thick white hair and worried face. I would tip-toe into the kitchen to make breakfast, expecting him to be fast asleep, slumped over the table, a pencil drifting out of his large hand. He was always awake, sitting straight in the chair, on his face the same indeterminable and unfathomable look as when we stood at the barrel while summer died all around us, watching the ash disappear into the thick grotto of whispering evergreens.

—What are you looking at? I asked, as I pulled up my chair and sat beside him. —What is happening? What do you see? I asked those questions every morning of him, never sure what I was really asking. Was I asking what he saw in the maps, or what he saw in the false autumn air? Every morning his answers were very different, and very much the same. Picking up a piece of onionskin paper covered in small diagrams and paragraphs thick with words, he would place it over the part of the town map to which it corresponded and point to a specific cluster of words or diagrams now floating over a specific building or street, I would ask the question, and he would speak.

—The B&I Circus Discount Emporium, along South Tacoma Way, where Mom used to buy my winter clothes?

—The woman found her children on the carousel, the one in the middle of the store. You remember it. Employees dressed as clowns, and a dying ape in a cage. She left the girl with the son, an older boy, while looking for a pair of boots that had a left and a right foot, and a pair of pants that had two legs instead of three.

Popcorn crackling and calliope music filled the air of the low-ceilinged acre-wide room. Cash registers and conversations. No one could have heard the screams. Maybe there were none. They all left their children there. She returned, all the parents returned, to a circular wood platform wobbling unevenly. Circus animals taffy-warped, the bodies of their children spiraling in ropes of blood and bone around wooden saddles, wooden poles, wooden stars. Store mannequins, plastic boys and girls with bright-eyed smiles, inserted like obscene arrows into delicate flesh. Calliope music, warped and stretched, washing through the air with their howls. Across the store, across a forest of metal clothing racks and rotting sales signs under a flickering fluorescent sky, the woman saw a store clown, bloated and swaying around a cement pillar like a dying parade float, slowly tearing the ape apart like cotton candy and cramming the pieces into its peppermint-striped mouth.

—The Safeway Supermarket, in the Highland Hills district, where you used to take me shopping when I stayed overnight with you and Granny?

—A young boy on a shopping trip with the mother of his best friend, who was playing in the refrigerated food aisles. Opening the doors, letting the frost collect on the warming surface, then drawing pictures and writing his name on the glass, like you used to do. His friend and mother were gone only for a few moments, looking for ice cream in another aisle. When they returned to the aisle, the young boy had vanished. Everyone was gone. No traces—no half-filled shopping carts, no purses or wallets on the linoleum floor, no cash registers open in half-completed transactions. The woman saw the boy's words behind glass, the last letter elongated as if the hand writing it had slid down and away. She opened the door. Behind the milk bottle shelves and the thick strips of plastic curtaining, the movements of something quiet and colossal. A thick stench of sweet decay blossomed out into the aisle, hitting the woman so hard that she turned as if slapped, vomiting on herself as she ran from the store, ran from displays molding and blackening on the shelves, ran from open bins of vegetables exploding in clouds of insects and spores, ran from meat that slithered and whispered as it burst from its packaging, dissolving and reforming into something greater than the sum of its blood and gristle and bone, something that might have vaguely resembled a monstrous, profane, and profoundly damaged reconstruction of the missing young boy.

—Point Defiance Park, at the northernmost end of Old Town, where Mom and Dad took me to see the old fort, and the animals at the zoo? Mom got sick there one time. She said it was the hot dogs. We never went back.

—You were too young to understand. They took you along the road that winds through the old-growth forest, called Five Mile Drive, up to the abandoned logging camp. They took you to the small unpaved street of wood plank houses and shops, to the remnants of the railroad tracks where a single steam engine car sat for a century, its giant blackened pistons and wheels locked tight with rust and rain, the engine car your mother rested in while your father took you to the fort. Day and night, now, park rangers hear the thunder and roar of the engine, blasting and crushing and consuming its way through the woods, leaving behind two deep oily grooves of blistered burning earth that no normal plant or tree will grow in again. Other things are found in the self-made tracks, things the rangers have taken their axes to, then buried deeper in the ground. The desiccated remains of animals, lions and orcas, polar bears turned inside out, their bones splintered and shot through with iron splinters. Bubbling jellicular mounds of placenta, slick and hot with blood, the aborted machine-like creatures within them tearing feebly at the thick membrane with inverted limbs and jaws. The entire park has been shut down, but eventually, everything once alive within it will be eaten and rebirthed as something else. After that, who knows where it will go. There's nothing to keep it from leaving.

—Narrows View, in the University Place School District.

Our district. My fingers traced wild ink spirals over to my old elementary school, just a block away from our house. My mother used to walk me up to the corner every day, then watch as I made my way halfway down the block then across the two-lane road, walking carefully within the thick white lines of the crosswalk. I used to imagine that if I stepped out of the lines and onto the worn black surface of the road, I would sink into a river of soft blacktop and tar, be pulled under even as my classmates continued across the wide parking lot and onto the breezeway that connected each of the ten low buildings that made up the school. They would run and dash through bright orange painted metal doors, disappear down linoleum-lined hallways into warm and humid classrooms, shedding coats and fluttering into chairs like autumn leaves. Bells would ring out, harsh and long clanging that echoed over the rooftops and trees, and the heavy yellow buses would belch smoke and squeal out of the parking lot and down the road; and then silence. And I, slowly sinking in the road, my school just yards away, my hands outstretched as if I could grasp it. I couldn't. I never could. And my mother, standing at the crooked red stop sign at the top of our little street, hands at her side, the edges of her brown coat flapping in the cold morning air, watching expressionless as I screamed, then pleaded, then struggled, then gave up and stopped moving at all, just watched her watching me, watching the whole world around us grow dark and still, until we were both trapped in an endless moment in time, never to grow old, never to live, never to die. My hands, forever outstretched for her help. Her eyes, forever burrowing out hollows in mine.

I lifted my fingers from the map. The tips were so blue with ink, it looked like they were rotting away.

—They found a girl in the road, my grandfather began. His large hand covered mine, and placed it back down on the map. He looked so tired, so old. —The skeleton of a large girl, a colossal girl, a giantess. Rising up from the blacktop. Bones like deformed corkscrews, each bone fused from the skeletons of many smaller girls.

—Not different girls, I said, slipping my hand away. —The same girl, trapped in the same part of the road a hundred thousand times. Layers of the same girl, trapped over and over again from kindergarten to sixth grade. Seven years, ending only last spring.

—Yes. My grandfather rose from the table, and started to fold up the maps and diagrams before my mother came downstairs. He didn't have to ask me how I knew.

***

My grandfather abandoned his maps not long after that. It wasn't that he lost interest. So many incidents occurred, it became useless to record them all. All put together, the entire town became an incident, and the map drowned beneath the network of inky words and roads, until all that remained of white paper was the tiny dot we called home. I don't think either one of us could bear to fill in that small, lonely white circle. We knew it would happen. My grandfather placed everything in the trash can barrel at the side of the yard one day, and we watched it curl into grey ash and float away in the sweet hot air. And after a while, no one remembered what day it was, or what week, or whether the season was fall or winter or spring. It was all the same season, the same day. I woke up to the same ghostly, lifeless images on the television as the day before, dressed for a school day I wouldn't recall going to by evening's end, when I sat at my desk, looking through books and papers for homework I never found.

And then one afternoon, although which afternoon of which month of what year it was, I would never know, my grandfather didn't come home. He left early in the morning for his job at the electric and water company as he always had, his soft grey fedora over his white hair, a thermos of milky coffee tucked into his briefcase. He kissed me on the forehead and told me to be safe, then drove off in the large car he had bought years ago when he became supervisor. I got ready for school, but I can't say if I went or not. The day passed, like all the days, in a soft haze of warmth and numbing sweetness that festered into early evening; and then the sun was pushing long bands of shadow and sun through the windows, over the dinner table. My grandfather would never abandon me. He wasn't coming home, I realized, because he couldn't; and the shock and sorrow of it sent something cold and hard trickling through my veins, and for the first time in what seemed like forever, I felt I was awakening from a terrible, suffocating dream.

—Are we going to wait for Puda? I asked my mother.

My mother set the casserole dish on the table, and stared at me. In her face, traces of what I might become, in another time, in another town. Her eyes, bright and furnace dark. Unbearable and all-consuming; and in her pupils I saw the small reflection of myself sink into the road a million times. I knew her answer then, before she said it.

—No.

She poured me a glass of lukewarm milk, and sat down. We ate in silence. The shadows lengthened until there was no more sun, and in my mind, I saw my gentle grandfather filling in that one remaining dot of white on his map with ink as blue as his eyes. And then he, too, was gone.

The next morning was not the same as all the other mornings. In the sleepy-sweet air, I dressed for classes I knew I had never attended, and never would, for friends and teachers I had never met or seen. Silvery thin men and women danced and fought in the snow of a television set that had long ago lost its cord. Images that did not exist. Everything in the world around me, a perverted misremembering, a suffocating lie. I put my schoolbooks under my bed, then changed my mind and stuffed them into the backpack. I had wanted to go, I had wanted to learn. I wanted to grow up. I had wanted the pale young man with the red-rimmed, pool-black eyes.

In the kitchen, my mother folded the top of my paper bag lunch as I drank my lukewarm milk. She licked the palm of her hand and ran it across my hair as I stared at the empty surface of the table, where my grandfather's hands had drawn rivers of blue ink over the map of my life. Her breath was whisper-cloying, as though I had walked into a web. In the distance, a train sounded out, mournful and low and long. I stared up at the ceiling, watching small spores detach like faint candle sparks and float down through the thick amber air, wink out as they hit my face, my skin, the ground. Everyone had known that the town had been dying, long before I truly saw it. The ground trembled and buzzed beneath my feet. I thought of my grandfather and the pale young man, and my face grew porcelain-tight.

—I have to go to school, I whispered. Each word took a century to slip from my mouth, as slow as the dying spores.

—No, you don't. My mother clasped my hand in hers, hard, and I felt our bones shift and crackle, our skin cake and fuse together like velvet and mold.

—Let me go, I said.

—No, she said. —I don't have to.

—Yes, I said. —You do.

A century later or more, I pulled my hand from hers. Her fingers stretched like taffy, wriggled and dropped away. Centuries later, my other hand thrust my grandfather's pen at the pulsing hollow of her throat. Droplets hung in the air, ruby and indigo comets catching the light as they orbited our wounds. Outside, the sun fell and rose as many times as the stars in the sky, and in that epoch my mother curled back her cracking lips wider, wider until there was only teeth and the volcanic black of her open mouth. With each step back from her and away, she bloated and burst, exponential in rot, pushing away the flimsy walls of our home, her veined translucent flesh pulsing with all the unborn variants of my life pushing outward to be free. In the molasses air, I turned, a millennium spent directing my terror and trembling legs away and up to the end of our street. If I cried, time looped back and ate the tears before they fell from my eyes. Only the pounding of my heart, a beat for every revolution of the galaxy, only the echo of a footfall with every dying star, only my mother always behind me, exploding, grasping, expanding, only everywhere the low dark roar of thunder and never rain.

—*They found a girl in the road, my grandfather had begun, in another universe.* —*Bones like deformed corkscrews, each bone fused from the skeletons of many smaller girls.*

Down the street, past the crosswalk and the thick white lines, and after that each step was quicker, and the centuries burned away. I never looked back. I passed myself, stuck in the blacktop a hundred thousand times, the giantess made of a hundred thousand girls, each one falling apart and clattering to the ground. And I ran to the edges of my northern town and past it and slipped beyond into the world, as all the cold bright skeletons of who I could have been swarmed behind me, plunging into the quivering moist mountains of putrescent flesh that had birthed us all, sinking her into the road where she lost me, all of them dying within her desire like little miscarried dreams.

I never stopped running.

Neither did she.

***

I've lived in this southernmost town for many lifetimes now, having lived in many other towns, each further south than the last. But all of the towns of this world have succumbed, as I knew they would, and there are no more towns beyond this one. There is nothing beyond this one, except the vast southern ocean, fields of ice, cold skies, colder stars. Here, winter is a diamond-hard fist, and summer an impossible dream. Or so it used to be, when I first made my way here, centuries or eons ago. I feel her now, again, in the air, in my bones. The days have begun to blend into each other as they did in all the other towns, the minutes and months and years, and a numbing sweet languor warms and slows us down until we no longer know or care. Everyone has known that the town is dying, long before we could see it. But only I know the reason why. My mother is coming for her little girl, once again burning the world away until there is only us and the memories of us together, until there is only her memories of how it used to be, how it should have been. And there are no more towns left to hide in, no more versions or dreams of me left to fight.

So I sit at the window of my apartment in that southernmost town, watching leaves turn red and gold that had only for the first time yesterday been green, watching the sun wax fat and throw off the late summer sparks I knew so well when I lived in the northern town, feeling the air grow camphor-bloated warm and sickly sweet. I sit at my window, turning the pages of schoolbooks I'll never learn from, watching the buildings do what I have never done. They age, morph, change. They bloat, fuzz over, and release soft spores from fat cankers sagging off their rotting faces, they malform and reform, they become more familiar with each calcifying day. The southernmost town is disappearing, and the northern town is rising, again. A steam engine howls in the distance as it gobbles up the miles, and so much more. The townspeople's movements weaken, slow, stop. They fade and drift away like vapor. The face of the pale young man appears in the windows, sliding from the flickering edges of my sight into full view as the weeks pass: and then the day will come when he will stand in the street below, as he has stood in all the other dusty streets of all the other towns, his large black eyes fixed on me as the twin-beaked raven in his grasp grotesquely struggles to call out my name, all the names of the monsters of my mother's memories. Behind and around him, behind and around me, the fully formed streets of my childhood soon will stand, birthed out of the ruins of the southernmost town like a still-born giantess, a puppet of calcified dreams and bone, pulled into unwanted existence by the strings of someone else's desire. This, this is my mother's endless suffocating desire, slowing time down around us, winding it back, back, until it becomes the amber-boned river in which I am always and only her little girl, eternal and alone.

I place the blue pen at the small pale circle of my throat.

I can stop time, too.

THE MYSTERIES

1

I t is that unnameable time of a late December morning, that nighttime hour that bleeds into tired dawn. My great-great-great-great grandmother sits in the living room, in the dark. I hear the rustling of her ancient newspaper as she turns each delicate page. The furnace has shut down after its daily muted roar, and a distant tick sounds through the walls as the metal ducts contract and cool. Other than the paper's whispers, it is the only sound in the house.

In the same dark, around the corner, past the foyer, I stand in the middle of the hallway, in my stained nightgown and robe, the ones I left behind some fifteen years ago when I left this place, my childhood home. My mother's house, so lovely and modern and clean—before The Grand moved in and took over, like she takes over everything. The outline of my overweight body hovers in the large black-stained mirror at the end of the hall, by the always-locked front door. A distorted Pierrette with a marshmallow body and mouthless face. I raise my hand. A second later, the creature in the mirror reluctantly moves. I can't blame it, I know why. The Grand can't see me, but she knows I'm there. She reads in the dark. She outlines her lips bright red in the pitch black of windowless closets. She embroiders tiny, perfect stitches in absolute gloom. Even during the day, the curtains in all the rooms are drawn, the lamps turned off. —This is how it used to be, she tells me over and over again. —When I was a child, we didn't have electric lamps. We didn't have radios. There were no televisions or computers; we weren't compelled to entertain ourselves all day. We were self-contained. Everything we needed came out of ourselves, out of our own family. This is how it was in the world. This is how it will always be for me.

I open my robe and pull the nightgown up. If there is a demarcation between fabric and flesh, mercury and air, the creature and me, I cannot see it. I search for the familiar black triangle between my legs. Even that has vanished. I am no different than the bare, cream walls around me. Outside of us, nothing can be seen. Yet within—a carnelevare of the numinous, waiting for release. Everything I need will come out of me.

—What are you doing? The Grand calls out from the living room. —Are you up? As she speaks, I hear her sniffing me out, and my blood runs peppermint hot and cold. She likes it like that.

I let my nightgown drop, and shuffle and squint my way around the corner. Morning presses against the thick curtains, to no avail. Everything glows, but dimly so. Against the far corner of the couch she curls, a fragile mound of bones and skin dressed in soft, flowery clothes. The open newspaper obscures the upper half of her body. I see only legs and knife-sharp fingers, the leaves of dark print flapping back in between. Her feet are small and perfectly formed, with nails like mother-of-pearl. She hasn't walked in a hundred and fifty years. She hasn't needed to.

—Give your great grand a sweet breakfast kiss, she says, floating up from the cushions. The newspaper flutters to the floor.

2

—It's time, my sister said. Her voice poured out of the phone like poison.

—No. Not yet. No.

—The Grand is sending for you, she continued over me, as if she couldn't hear my voice.

—I don't want to go.

—You don't have a choice. Check your email—I sent the plane ticket to you already. You have a month to pack up and say goodbye.

—I have a life here.

—I had a life, too. And now I get it back. But only if you come. You know what happens to me if you don't. She'll use me up until there's nothing left.

—You know I'd never let that happen. But why so soon?

—She's tired of me. I don't please her anymore, or so she says. At any rate, I've done my time. It's your turn now.

—This is wrong. You know that.

—It doesn't matter. We can't change it. This is why we were born.

It was late summer, back then, and my city was a volcano of bright life. I took her call at work, in an empty corner office. I gave an obfuscated answer that pleased us both and hung up. Outside, day was racing down into the shimmery fires of night. Twenty floors down, clogged streets were transforming into long-running strands of rubies and diamonds, winding around buildings slick with coruscated light. I pressed my hand against the glass. Hard and hot. When I took my hand away, a thin film of perspiration remained, outstretched against the avenue as though trying to grasp it. The ghost hand of a ghost girl. Within seconds, it disappeared.

I said my goodbyes at work without telling them I'd never return, and bought boxes on the way home, just enough to ship a few piles of books and clothes. My small room in the SRO building didn't hold that much, anyway. I'd always known this moment would come, and so my decisions had already been made, years ago, how I would live my life and how I would defend it. I was more prepared than my sister could imagine, and more ruthless than The Grand could ever be. Desperation made me so. In a way, I was no different than her.

The next morning I settled my account at the SRO, made a stop at the post office, then walked twenty blocks south, down through my beautiful city. Past blight-tinged gentrification, past markets and parks and coffee shops and wide bustling avenues; and then west, over to the edge of the river, to block after block of monolithic warehouses and factories, moldering in shadowed silence and brick dust until their moment in history came again. It was like I'd walked this path just yesterday, even though a decade had passed. —When you've made your decision, be it tomorrow or a million tomorrows from now, you'll find us, he had said with his yellow-teethed smile as I looked over his exhibits and wares. —You won't ever need a map.

3

She leans into me in the queer morning light for her kiss, and my mouth slackens and my head lolls back. Every day is the same, and night no different than day. Darkness, rain needling against the rooftop and windows, wind thundering through distant trees. She never sleeps. Her need keeps her running hot and constant, a nuclear reactor of hunger that can never be shut down. —It's not so bad, my sister said, the few times I spoke with her until she stopped taking my calls. —She takes from you, but she gives you something back, in a way. It's almost an even exchange. —What does she do, what is she, how can she be? I asked over and over again. —Is she a vampire? A ghoul? An insect? Why do we submit?

—I don't know, my sister always replied. —Who can say?

Sometimes, at night, I awake in the dark and feel her hovering over me, a weight and emotion I sense but never feel or see. Paralyzed, I breathe all my damp terror and fear into the emptiness of my childhood room. Above, mote by mote she sucks it in. Sleep itself is no refuge. In my dreams I rise to the ceiling, my skin brushing against the faded outlines of spiraling galaxies my mother painted for me long ago. And then the ceiling, the stars, soften and yield—her arms are around me, mouth against mine, while in the waking world, my body moans and shivers, ten feet above my bed. The days are worse. I can't hide in my room forever, and so I venture out into the house, wandering like a restless ghost of myself through the still rooms. Everywhere, vestiges of the life I had before, of my sister and me as children, of my mother and the father I too briefly knew. Cobwebbed tableaus of toys and dishes. Photos of distant summers, succumbing to speckled mold. A faint scent of my mother's perfume rising like a tired ghost from a dresser of musty clothes. Old folders of school homework, boxes of books my aching eyes can no longer read in the ever-dim light. And I, always never knowing where she is, in what room, squeezed into what tight corner or closet or crack. Never knowing when she will ooze out and ignore me, or play with me, or pounce.

—You're different, she says this morning, her vulpine face hovering just above my head. —I don't like it. I smell animals. I smell fire and sugar and rust. The words wash over my face like gasoline fumes, and tears dribble out of my eyes into my mouth. My flesh grows heavy and prickly-numb. Her face is an amorphous stain, a blur. I open my mouth to speak. All that comes forth is a burp, loud and wet. Bile dribbles down my lips and chin. It tastes like rotting grapes.

The Grand recoils. —You're sick, she hisses. She hates any hint of illness or disease.

—No, I'm not, I garble. Thin pine needles slide out of my running nose and onto my tongue. —It's the carnival.

—You're delirious.

—It's coming.

—What are you talking about?

A slow, long tremor erupts throughout my belly. My tearing eyes shut tight, and I smile. I am horrifying and new. She leans back into me, curious. Lips and breath against my cheek, mouth open, seeking, seeking. —Tell me everything, she whispers. —Fill me up with everything.

I lift my wet nightgown. —Stay with me, and you can take everything you need.

I drop to the floor, back arched, thighs apart. The second contraction rips through me, and I howl. The barker said there would be pain, and he didn't lie. He said it would be the eighth wonder of the world.

4

The barker stood where I had seen him a decade ago, as if he had never moved from the spot: on a wood-planked platform in the middle of a vast dirt and sawdust-covered warehouse floor, surrounded by rows and rows of broken and abandoned caravans and carousels and fair rides in fading pastels, painted canvases depicting creatures and humans of sublime beauty and deformity, statues and stuffed beasts, tanks and cages, carts and costume-choked trunks. It took an eternity of footsteps to walk to him. The musk of animal and tang of sea creature and the green of chipped wood filled my lungs—none of it had moved in ten years, none of it had changed. Bits of jewel-colored glitter floated through the smoky, popcorn-scented air. Antiques, it said on the crumpled brochure I'd found blowing about on the street that spring day so long ago, and had carried in my purse ever since. Rare Circus Items Curated from America's Golden Age of Entertainment. Powerful Carnival Artifacts Rescued from Civilizations Lost Forever in the Mists of Time. A Veritable Cornucopia of Wonders, Mesmerizing and Terrifying. This Once in a Lifetime Opportunity, Only For You.

—Are you ready? he called out, and his words echoed back and forth between the high walls before dying out in a faint burst of calliope music. —Have you made your choice? He lifted his cane and pointed down. Below the stage sat a massive flat-topped megalith, with five black marble boxes resting on its rough surface, each carved on the top with the name of an ancient carnival, culled from histories lost forever, as the brochure had said. Within each box, though, anything but dry history resided. Chaos, essence, power, folding in on itself in infinite spirals. Waiting for an incubator, a warm walking womb to carry it to its new home, to release. Unchecked primal appetite, that could consume anything, even a woman with an endless appetite of her own. I felt my breath shallow out, my heart beat fluttery and weak.

I reached out and touched the box labeled *KRONIA*. It vibrated slightly under my fingertips. After a pause, I pushed it back.

—Masks and merriment, as I recall. Too weak, I said. The barker nodded and smiled.

I picked up the boxed labeled *NAVIGIUM ISIDIS,* and immediately placed it on top of the *KRONIA* box. —Floats, processionals, parades. I think she'd be amused. I don't want to amuse her.

At the far edge of the floor, a chair moved. I felt the contents of the space shifting, as if rousing itself from a too-long dream. A low sigh wafted across the room, or perhaps it was only the wind, or the ghost of a dream of the wind.

Three boxes were left on the stone. —*BACCHANALIA,* I said, picking up the one to the left. I placed it on top of the stack. —Savage. She'd be disoriented, repulsed. But not incapacitated.

—Are you certain, madam? the barker said. —Wine-soaked madness and lust in the night? Nothing to stop you from partaking as well, if you desire. If you aren't dismembered, that is.

But I had moved on. *SATURNALIA,* said the next box. I lifted it up.

—What's this one again?

—Pageants. Very theatrical, said the barker. — I must warn you: there will be many, many clowns.

I added *SATURNALIA* to the stack. A single box remained. *DIONYSIA,* it said. I ran my fingertips over the carved letters. The barker smiled.

—Great festivities within, he said. —A carnelevare of god-frenzied transformation, which subsumes and liberates all.

—I don't want to transform her, I said, adding the box to the stack. —I don't want to liberate or destroy her.

For the first time, the barker looked unsure. —What is it that you want, then?

—I want something so wondrous and primal, she'll never be able to leave it. I want to fill her up, completely. I want her to fall in love.

The warehouse floor grew quiet. —There are no boxes left, the barker said. —There are no more choices.

I reached out, placing both hands flat on the megalith as I contemplated the stack. The stone was warm and smooth, except for spider-thin scratches. I moved my fingers over them. Back and forth. A sixth name, in a language I did not recognize, running across the surface. A secret, sixth carnelevare.

—No more choices, the barker repeated.

—There never was a choice. This is the one I've always wanted, I said. —The carnival with no name.

—The first. Do you know what it is you're asking for? The barker motioned to the dusty rides and ruins scattered across the warehouse floor. —It won't be like any of these. No sequins or carousels or quaint colored lights.

I pointed to the black boxes. —The other carnivals I considered were nothing like that.

The barker's cane came to rest on the pitted surface of the megalith. A sharp click hit the air. —Nothing since the dawn of history has been like this.

I said nothing. There was nothing more to say. After a time, the barker nodded.

—As you wish, he said. —The conception will be—complex. I will need time.

—I have thirty days.

—Thirty days out there, you mean. He pointed up, to pale blue skies shimmering outside the high windows. —In here, it will be as long as I need it to be.

—All right.

—I am compelled to caution you: your body will change. Your mind will change. And there will be pain.

—I'm a woman. There always is.

5

Outside the house, days have come and gone. Months have bled away. Within these walls, the universe pauses to watch.

In the undiscovered country of my torso, from out the limit-less valleys of my most intimate self, another monster emerges, another child of the carnelevare, horns and hooves slicing through skin and muscle and bone and capillaries. By my side, The Grand struggles, but I do not lessen my grip. Massive clawed hands clutch at my slick thighs, hoisting its heavy furred body up and out and into a room so spattered by my blood that I cannot tell where my body ends and where the house begins, except there is no begin-ning and ending, it is all one and the same, an ouroboros of con-tinual birth. And the monster cleans its bull-shaped face against my stomach and licks my breasts, and crawls away, far into the house, and something else begins to emerge from my body, worse or better I cannot tell. This is the sixth carnelevare, the great re-moving and raising of the flesh, the coming of a god so old it does not remember its name, and with it all its attendants beautiful and hideous, bursting forth from every orifice of my flesh to celebrate the mystery of all mysteries.

The floor beneath me shudders beneath my sudden burgeon-ing weight, and I hear the crackling of tree limbs, the cracking of bones. The dislocation of my jaw, the colossal clang of bells. Vastness pours out of me like an ocean. And the backwash of dark-ness rolls over my mind like a breaking wheel, and I float in the spirals of those faded painted galaxies of my childhood, holding my great-great-great-great grandmother's slender hand. Who lives around all those stars, can they see us, what are their names, my nine-year-old self asks her as the ghost of my mother daubs specks of gold and silver paint across the fathomless blue, and my grandmother replies, I am the only human in the world who will ever know.

Together we look up, and up, and up, and from our starry perch we see the deep woods of all the worlds, the labyrinths and groves, we see the satyrs and stags and bulls and the wolves and women and men. Masked and naked, they dance and contort around frightened fires, they chant their prayers and pleas into the shadowed cracks of the world, they laugh and crash together in god-fevered horror and cry out as the sparks of their devotion float up and wink out with their ecstasy. They gyre together and pull apart transformed, endless variations of monstrosities kaleidoscoping out of their frenzied couplings. And I am the night, and out of the night and the woods their god comes to them, into them, into her, in the strike of lightning and the shuddering of the earth, in the terminal vastation of his song.

—Close your eyes, I whisper.

—Never.

I sigh, and the fires wink out one by one. I sink back down to the floor, to a room filled with clear light and the silk rattle of morning through the tree's wintery bones.

I force my sticky eyelids open. My body feels empty, still. I blink, and the ceiling swims in a thin wash of red. I can't tell if I'm dead or alive. I'm not breathing, and I cannot feel the beating of my heart. There is no pain, I realize in shock: the complete absence of such an all-consuming presence makes me light, free. I roll slightly, slowly, and sit up. I am covered head to toe in blood, and I am whole. My right hand holds the mangled, broken wrist of a woman's severed arm, the grip so tight and deep beneath her flesh that I cannot see my fingertips. Crimson-brown gobs of placenta and blood cover every inch of our joined skin. Under the drying gore, I recognize The Grand's flower-carved wedding ring. I leave the ring on the couch, with the arm.

Outside, gossamer trails of night-blue mist waft through the backyard like torn strands of the Milky Way, sparking with millions of little pinpricks of pure white light. They drift and catch on the sleeping faces of the women and men pulled from their neighboring homes in the carnelevare's orgiastic wake, settle into their hair and over their bare tangled limbs, crash and break apart against tall pine trees and dissipate with the rising sun. A thread of it trails against my bare leg, disappearing beneath the triangle of matted hair. The effluvium of a nameless carnival as it blew in and out of town. I gently pull it out and let it float away.

At the edge of the yard, legs tucked under thighs white and hard as marble, the small body of a woman with a missing left arm rests under a large tree. I walk over, and kneel before The Grand. She looks no older than me. Her pale green eyes are open, wide, blank. They stare through and beyond me, up into the sky. Her face is raised and lips are parted, as if being forced to drink from a bottomless cup. Or perhaps, as if about to speak a name.

6

A blood-orange sun was sinking slowly into the edges of my city's wide electric edges, and I raised my worshiping hands and face like a grateful Akhenaton into its early autumn heat. I had lost a month, and so much more. It was time to go home, all the way home. Behind me, just within the shadows of the open warehouse doors, behind the boundary he could not see or cross, the barker stood, hesitant.

—What does it feel like? he asked.

—This? I turned, hand on my stomach, already slightly curved.

—That. All of it, the god and the power and the mysteries, folded into something so small and insignificant as you. To be so full. And, the sun. The weight of the air on your body. The pleasure of bearing so much pain. Being a part of the world, while knowing you're not really a part of anything at all.

—I couldn't tell you. I don't have any answers.

He stared at me, waiting, disappointed yet still expectant; and then his eyes glazed. I could see him moving beyond me, his mind traveling to that invisible realm beyond the carnelevare's end, where all questions are answered, all hunger sated, where all the endless pleasurable and terrifying variations of the chase dwindle down to a dead and desiccated end.

—Do you really want to know?

He looked up into the sky, then smiled his yellow-teethed grin.

—No.

THE LAST, CLEAN, BRIGHT SUMMER

This Journal Belongs To:
Hailie

Tacoma, June 15th

I'm writing this in the car. Mom cried again this morning when we left the house. Everything was spotless and put away just like we were going on a vacation for a little while, even though we're not coming back until late fall. She'd been cleaning like crazy since last year, like literally starting on my fourteenth birthday. Dad says she's nesting, because when we come back home, it'll be with a new baby brother, and maybe a sister too. Which totally shocked me, because I didn't even know she was pregnant. There were so many things she wanted to take, but Dad wouldn't rent one of those big RV's, and everything had to fit in our crappy old VW camper instead. So she just made everything look super neat and nice. I swear, I did more laundry and dishes in the last month than in the last five years! Anyway, so we packed two suitcases and one large backpack each, and got rid of most of the food that might spoil, except for what we're taking (which is currently sitting in paper bags and boxes next to me on the back seat, and all around my feet), and that's it. We pulled out of the driveway early this morning, before it was really light, and I turned around and watch my little yellow house disappear. Last night Dad went out into the backyard with Abby, our dog, to the spot in the back where Alex was. That was the only time I cried.

And now we're on our way down the freeway to Olympia. Dad isn't taking the longer scenic way around the peninsula, but it'll still be a couple of days before we get to the town (which has almost NO internet access, of course), so I brought this journal (even though I'm totally lazy about writing in it) and a couple books. We're going to Oceanside for a humungous family reunion—I was born there, and so was my mom. My parents moved away when I was born, but we used to go back every summer until five years ago, when my younger brother died and my mom said she couldn't do it anymore, at least for a while. I remember we stayed at a really cute cottage inland from Oceanside, a kind of suburban area called the Dunes, where my mother's aunt used to live. She would babysit us while my parents went to the parties—we were always too young to go. I remember it was all shiny wood, and Great Auntie had two huge trunks, one filled with puzzles, and one filled with the most beautiful dolls. And if you stood in the road outside her driveway, you could see past the houses and scrubby trees all the way to the ocean, even though it was almost a mile away. That's how flat it is. That's why the reunion is held there, Dad says, because of the strong tides and the flat beach. Mom doesn't like to talk very much about it. I know she's never liked the reunions, but I'm kind of looking forward to it. I just hope there'll be some interesting boys in town.

Aberdeen, June 16th

This town is super creepy, but kind of cool in that weird way. Mom says all the geometry of the architecture here is wrong, and it makes everyone depressed. I have no idea what that means. We stayed the night in a motel just off the highway, and I kept waking up to all the traffic sounds. So, after Mom and Dad were asleep for a while, I got dressed and snuck outside. We were the only ones checked in, and all the other windows were dark. I could see the highway from the balcony, all the lights of the trucks and cars. I just stood there in the dark for a while, listening to the sound of all those cars, watching the red lights stream constantly away.

And then I saw them. I don't know where they came from, but it was like all of a sudden they were just there, standing under the bright yellow parking lot lights. It was two faceless men, although I could barely tell. They were naked except for very tall black top hats, with very shimmery pale skin, all scales, I think, or maybe skin like an alligator. I was so shocked I almost peed my pants! I just stood there frozen, and my skin got all hot and cold like it does when you're so frightened you can't move. They stood there too, looking up at me. I thought about running, but Dad had said that they weren't dangerous. Just be respectful, and think of them as our summer observers, he had said. Just let them watch us, and we'll all get along just fine. And then they started walking very slowly and gracefully across the parking lot, and I don't know why I did this, but I waved, in a very slow and dignified arc. And they both waved back! I was so happy. And then they disappeared, and I stood there a while longer, watching the cars' lights twinkling and all the stars rush past me overhead. It was a pretty good night.

This morning before we left Aberdeen, we had breakfast at the restaurant downtown that we used to go to all the time when we came down here, in the old brick building near the factories Dad would visit as part of his job. We all had that awesome french toast, just like we used to, and Mom asked the cook for his secret recipe, and he said no, just like he used to. And then they got in a fight, and Mom was all like, I don't know why you won't give it to me since we're probably the last customers you'll have all summer, and he was all like, well, summer's not over yet and besides, in

the fall I'm heading down to South America and taking my recipe
with me, and then she was all, it's not South America anymore,
you idiot, who do you think is left down there who eats french
toast, and then she ran off to the bathroom. The cook grew super
angry and quiet, and then my dad took him aside, probably to
apologize and tell him Mom's all hormonal and everyone down in
Obsidia will totally love his secret french toast.

Mom needs to chill out. She explained what's going to happen
at the reunion, that we have to dance around some big-ass dying
sea creature in some ancient tribal ceremony to honor our ances-
tors, and throw some spears into it to "defeat" it, and it's totally
not going to be hard at all. It sounds stupid and completely lame.

The Dunes, Oceanside, June 23rd

We're at the cottage now. It's been kind of a strange couple of days.
I'm kind of bored and anxious and I don't know. I guess just it's
weird to feel like you're on summer vacation when something so
incredible and important is going to happen and you finally get to
take part. Mom and Dad are in the town on a dinner date, and this
is the first chance I've really had to myself. We got to Oceanside
on the 16th. It's straight up the coast from Ocean Shores, but it's
a long drive, and the highway gives out to dirt roads and logging
roads after a while, and those are a bit hard to find. There were
less cars, though. People up here are like us, they're relatives, part
of the family or they're company people like Dad who are cool
about everything and stay out of our way. We didn't stop at Ocean
Shores, even though I wanted to, but Dad said it was off limits because they'd already done their ceremony and totally fucked it up
(his swear word, not mine!) and the town was a total mess. We did
stop at this really awesome beach further up the coast, just outside
this huge area of abandoned quarry pits. It's hard to describe how
the ocean was there. I mean, there were these waves that were so

high and grey and hard, you could feel the beach quake when they crashed down, and they sounded like thunder. They would rise up in the air, and just hang there like they were alive, like they were waiting. For what, I don't know. All the sand was pure black, just like in parts of Hawaii, and we found a skeleton of some huge whale thing that was about as long as our old neighborhood road. Dad kept calling it a kraken, which was hilarious. Mom got pretty excited when she saw it, and took all kinds of pictures and had us all pose next to the skull. I sat in the eye socket. Yeah, it was kind of neat! I was just happy to see Mom so happy. It was sunny and warm out, and there were gulls everywhere and the funniest looking crabs.

Anyway, so we got to Oceanside in the late afternoon, when the sun was setting over the Pacific and the sky was pink and orange and red, and the air smelled all sandy and salty like brine. Dad drove down the main street and parked next to the chowder house where we'd have dinner, and we got out and stood in the middle of the road. Just like near the cottage, you'd usually be able to see all the way to the ocean, it would look like the road just kept going on through the beach and then under the waves. Except, not anymore, because of the wall. Dad's a really important architect and he helped design this, for Oceanside and for other towns all up and down the coast that are having family reunions, for whenever it's their time. Except Ocean Shores, of course, and a couple other places that didn't build a wall and got destroyed. Mom took more pictures, and then we went inside.

We got to the cottage after dark. It was exactly like I remembered it, all the nautical stuff everywhere and the flowered couch that turns into a bed. Mom got teary-eyed when she saw the trunks of toys, but she covered it up and fussed around in the kitchen with the food while Dad and I pretended not to notice. I'll admit, I got a bit sad when I saw the puzzles, too. I remember Alex and me putting them together on the rickety cardboard table Great Auntie set up for us. That was the last summer before he started getting sick. It was the inoculations. All the men in our family start taking it when they're about nine, to fight some infection they're not immune to when they grow up, but sometimes they'd have allergic reactions to it, and it would do terrible things to their bodies, like it did to Alex. Dad felt so guilty, but how could he have known?

Anyway, it's been quiet. There aren't any interesting boys here at all, they're all at the wall, I guess, along with the men. I've been spending the days with my mom, and some of the other relatives and their daughters, who I guess are my cousins, reading and getting a tan in their yards. No one cool is around here. None of my cousins are interesting. One girl didn't even know who Beyoncé was! I brought my good bikini for nothing.

The Wall, Oceanside, July 5th

Yesterday was the 4th, of course, and all over the Dunes there were lots of backyard parties and barbeques. I finally met a few cute boys, but they were all my cousins, of course, and they wouldn't even talk to me and were pretty rude. Of course, we all ate dinner in the afternoon, because when it got dark, everyone in the town and from the Dunes met at the wall. It was insane. We all walked down the long main road, no one was in their car, and none of us were allowed to bring our cameras or phones. Most of the lights were off except for some crazy lamps in a few store and restaurant fronts, these large circles of glass that glowed a deep green. They were so pretty and strange. I kept looking down at my skin—it looked like it was being lit from inside. All the women and the girls looked like that. All the boys and men were dressed in black suits, even though it was really hot. I mean, this is the middle of summer, after all. A lot of them didn't look very happy about it. But it's tradition, Dad says. It's part of the reunion. And another tradition is that this was the one night all the men escorted the women to the top of the wall, the only time we were allowed to be up there. Well, I'm sure the tradition started out as another night, but having it on the Fourth of July probably gave them an excuse for all the fireworks and beer.

When we got to the wall, the men escorted us single file inside, up these long narrow corridors of stairs that go to the top. It was kind of like a school fire drill in reverse. There were no lights in the stairs, and I pretty much had to climb them with my hands and feet like a dog. I have no idea who was behind me, but I'm glad they couldn't see my butt in their face. When we got to the top, there were about ten observers waiting for us like the ones I saw in the parking lot, naked and faceless with high top hats. I couldn't tell if some of them were the same ones from the parking lot. They didn't look so friendly close up. Everyone grew really quiet and still. We all stood in line around the curved edge, all the women in front so they could see over the metal railing, and the men behind them. I wanted to see the town because we were so high up, but the guy behind me grabbed me and forced me to turn back around. What an asshole.

Anyway. We all stood there for a few minutes, in the dark. If we were supposed to be looking at something, no one said. No one spoke. The beach was black, with that same sand Dad and Mom and I had found by the quarry site, but here it was smooth and completely bare. I didn't realize how high the wall was, but it's enormous, so wide that all of us—maybe close to a thousand people—can stand on it, and the beach that it circles around is huge. The waves were further back than I remember, or at least further back than they are by the Dunes, and they were massive. I was shocked. If they'd been any closer, they would have come right over the wall. They would rush in toward the wall like a herd of gigantic animals, like serpents made out of water and foam, and I felt everyone sort of gasp and shrink back all at once, me included, and then they'd come crashing down, dragging the sand away and leaving the beach smooth and clean.

So we watched for a few more minutes, and then the fireworks started over the town, and everyone turned to the other side of the wall and oohed and awed. It was a pretty good show. I kept turning back to the beach, though. Having my back to those waves made me a bit nervous. I bent over the railing slightly to get a better view of the beach and the bottom of the wall. I don't know how we're expected to get down there for the ceremony— I couldn't see any stairway openings, and the wall goes right into the ocean, for a really long way. Maybe we take boats around the edges? I don't know. And then the fireworks were over and everyone went back down the steps. There were some parties in town, at the bars and restaurants, but Mom and Dad went home with me instead. The neighbors down the road were having a big pool party, which seems really redundant (having a pool, that is) when you live next to the ocean but whatever, so I knew they'd go there. Mom asked me if I had any questions about the beach, and I said no, but I was lying. I don't know, I didn't want to talk about it. Mom put her arm around me and said everything would be fine. Funny, when just three weeks ago she was the one having complete kittens about the reunion.

When we got to the edge of the Dunes, Dad tapped my shoulder and told me to look around. All along the wall, those green globe lamps had been placed. You could see this huge curve of weird green lights hovering in the air between the town and the beach, all of them flashing like little lighthouse beacons or the lights along a runway. He asked me if I thought that was cool and I said yeah, awesome, or something like that. And that's when I really started to bug out about this whole reunion thing, and felt my skin grow all hot and cold and shivery again, although I acted like I was totally chilled out and fine.

Here's the thing. When I was staring out at the ocean, when everyone else was looking at the fireworks, I saw something. I swear I saw something. Way far off in the ocean, past all the waves, it was in the moonlight, just for a second, and then it was gone. It wasn't an orca or a blue whale, I've seen those tons of times before. I swear to god I saw a gigantic hand.

The Dunes, July 11th

Nothing has been happening. I guess it'd be a great vacation, if it were a vacation, if I didn't have this constant ball of anxiety inside that makes me double over in pain every once in a while. It's really hot now, almost 85 every day. I go to the neighbor's house most days, and lay on a blanket by the pool listening to my iPod or reading. I've got a great tan. Mom goes with me and gossips with the other women, or sometimes we'll go into Oceanside and just walk around, shopping for trinkets or clothes at the little stores, buying magazines, eating lunch at the one cafe. When we're out-side, walking down the narrow sidewalks, I'll try so hard not to, but I always look up at the wall. I can't help it. The lights are still flashing, day and night, and sometimes there's a huge booming sound and the ground shakes a little, like the waves are reaching the wall and trying to knock it down. Most of the men from the town and the Dunes are up there, and a lot of observers, too. Dad spends every day there. He doesn't talk about it, and I am so re-lieved that he doesn't. We'll have dinner—Mom's teaching me how to cook, I made spaghetti last night!—and then we'll watch TV if the reception is good, or play board games, or go over to a relative's house and hang out. No one talks about the wall. Sometimes I'll look up and catch a bunch of Mom and Dad's friends or relatives looking at me, and they'll stop talking and look away. They do this with all the girls. Super creepy.

Last night I snuck outside and tried to take a picture of the lights, but something's wrong with my phone, it doesn't work at all. I think it's broken. This summer blows.

The Dunes, July 23rd

I'm so tired, but I can't get to sleep. Dad just left. It's about mid-night, and maybe about an hour ago, some men knocked on the door, and Dad spoke with them for a few minutes, and then he changed into his black suit and left. He told us it's almost time, and to get a good night's sleep, and early tomorrow morning the men would come for us and the ceremony would begin. I kind of freaked out a little, but Mom calmed me down, then she poured us both a small glass of wine—my first ever!—and she got all teary-eyed again and gave a little speech about how everything was going to change and tomorrow I was going to become a woman (GOD! so embarrassing) and how she was so proud of me and that she knew that no matter what happened, someday I'd be a wonderful mom. The wine tasted terrible, I thought wine was sup-posed to taste like fruit, but she made me drink the whole glass. I feel a little gross now, kind of floppy and fuzzy. I keep thinking about Alex. I think about his skeleton, under our backyard, all twisted and spiraled and decayed. And Abby, my big-eyed pug, her little skull filled with worms and dirt.

Why do all the men wear top hats?

Why do I hear horns

The Dunes, August 29th

Wow. I lost a month.

The cast has been off my arm for a couple of days now, and even though the fingers are a bit stiff, I can finally write again without bursting into tears. When I say that, I mean I can write without my fingers hurting, and I can write about what happened without tears rolling down my face, without dropping my pen to the floor, staring off into space, at the wall, through the window, staring anywhere except my journal, where I have to remember what happened and put it into words. Which I guess we're not supposed to do—that is, the women aren't supposed to do this, make records of anything. But I think I should, for reasons I won't go into just right now. I just think it's important to remember, to have a record of my own. Mom and Dad have gone into town for the afternoon to check on my new sisters, so I'm all alone.

So this is what happened.

THE BEACH, July 24th

I don't remember falling asleep. It was the wine, Mom explained later. The men put a little something in it to help us sleep. It just makes it easier for everyone.

I woke up in a cage, naked. My head was against Mom's thigh, and she was stroking my hair like she used to when I was a little girl. The cage was iron or steel, and it was covered with thick canvas and fastened underneath the bottom, so you couldn't lift it or see outside no matter which way you looked. I could smell the salt of the ocean, and hear the rumble of waves. I knew we were outside, right on the beach, but it sounded far away, like at low tide in the morning. I felt really disoriented, I sat up and tried to ask Mom what was happening, but she shushed me. She was naked, too. I was so embarrassed, I wanted to die. Then she whispered to keep quiet, and just do everything she and the other women did. She said if we got separated and I got confused or afraid, my instincts would tell me what to do.

The canvas rose up—and the smell hit us, not just of the ocean but the low tide stench of something leviathan and dying. I heard a couple girls vomit. The wall was on one side of our cages, and the beach on the other. It was early morning, so early that the sand and water and sky looked all the same color, sort of a flat dark blue. Something was on the beach, white and malformed. I guess I thought it was a whale at first—what else could be that big? And then I realized it was an ocean liner—no whale could be that huge. Mom pushed at the cage, and one side swung open. All around us, against the curve of the wall, cages were opening, and women and their daughters were stepping out onto the sands, maybe five hundred of us in all. We were all barefoot, and all naked and shivering in the cool air. I squinted and turned my head, and that's when I realized. It was so large, I hadn't recognized it at first. But then, yes. I'd seen it before.

It was a woman. A woman so massive I couldn't see the ends of her legs. They were still in the water, the waves lapping at her knees. Her arm was stretched out, fingertips almost touching the row of cages. That was the hand I knew I'd seen at the ocean's edge that night, pale and grasping in the distant moonlight. We started to walk down the beach toward her face, some of us running. Long blue-green hair like seaweed, spread across the black beach. She lay on her back, face to the side, saucer-wide eyes open. She didn't look like some hideous fish creature. She looked like any of us. She looked like me. I could feel the heat of her breath. She was beached but alive, barely. And her stomach! It rose up like Mount Rainier, white and round and full.

She's pregnant, I whispered to Mom, and she nodded. *Are we supposed to dance around her?* I asked.

Not quite. We have to help her give birth, she replied. *But before that, we need to be brave. There's something very difficult we need to do.*

An object slid off the woman's belly and dropped onto the sands. I almost didn't see it at first, it was the same color as her mottled flesh. It rose up from the sand, and everyone jumped back a bit. Another object slid down her belly, and one more slithered out from under her breast. All across her body, I could see movement, hundreds of ripples breaking free. Mom grabbed my arm, hard, so I couldn't run. All around me, the women were whispering to the girls, holding their arms.

Don't fight them, Mom whispered. *And don't run. Just let them do what they need to do.*

What are they, I asked.

I don't know. Maybe the men know. They ride her body up to the surface of the ocean, and now they're waiting for her babies to be born.

Babies? I asked.

She has eggs, hundreds of female eggs, and when they hatch, they'll be waiting for the girls.

To eat them, I said?

No, Mom said. *To spawn.*

From beside me, a high-pitched scream. I saw a girl break free and start to run, and then we all screamed, the thin sounds bouncing back and forth across the wall. I punched my mother in the stomach and pushed her away. We all ran, we ran as fast as we could across the soft slow sands back to the cages and it didn't make any difference, none of us were fast enough and none of us were strong and something grabbed my hair and flipped me up high in the air like one of my auntie's dolls. I came down flat on my back, and it was on me in a flash, soft squishy skin and sucking mouth and the smell. And it was hammering into me, with its huge hard lumpy thing that hurt so much I cried and threw up, and it licked my face and stuck its flappy tongue in my mouth and I threw up some more and choked and it just wouldn't stop pounding against me and I felt my right wrist snap under its grip, and the sudden pain made everything bright and calm and clear. I lay still, and the creature fucked me over and over and I looked up at the iron sky and waited for the sun to break over the wall.

And after a while it stopped, and rolled off me, shuddering and flopping like a giant fish. I lay on the sands with my legs open, mouth open, watching it die. All around me, girls and women were fighting and screaming, the grunts and groans filling the air, the smell of rancid water and vomit and semen and chum. Everyone sobbed. I sat up, slowly. Every muscle in my body hurt, every bone felt broken or bruised. Already half of the creatures were dying or dead. Some were fighting viciously over girls, tearing off each other's limbs with thick claws and lantern-jawed teeth. I didn't know where my mother was, but I didn't want to look. Next to me, a girl lay half buried in the sand. I recognized her from the Dunes. Her head was caved in, the dead creature's thing still resting in the broken nest of teeth spilling out of her mouth.

I would have thrown up again, but I was completely empty inside.

Behind me, the cages started to clatter. I turned around, keeping my head low. Large knives were falling onto the tops of the cases, some of them bouncing onto the sands. Long sharp butcher knives and machetes. Nets followed, huge fishing nets slithering down like punctured balloons. I stared up at the wall. In the growing light, I could see some of the men hurling the knives down the long curve of stone. The rest of them stood at the railing, writing notes in books, talking to the observers, staring down at us through telescopes and binoculars. And then I saw. Most of the men had their penises out. They were masturbating. They were watching us, watching their wives and their daughters scream and break apart and die on the beach just like that giantess, and they were masturbating through the metal rails as if it were the most exciting thing in the world.

I felt a hand on my foot, and I whipped my leg back, swallowing my scream. My mother, crawling past me. *Grab a knife and a net,* she said. *We have to harvest the eggs.* I watched her move past me, blood on her broken nose, blood trickling between her legs. *My arm is broken,* I said. *Then use your other arm.* She threw a machete at me, and it landed against my legs, slicing open my skin. I glared at her, but she just walked past. I followed her, limping, tears running down my face. *That's for the punch in the stomach,* she finally said.

When does the dancing start, I said.

Don't start that shit with me, she replied. She didn't look back, only kept walking toward the giantess. The other older women were limping and crawling to the cages, grabbing knives, helping the younger girls get up, heading down to the large stomach. Some of them were walking around, sticking their knives into the creatures that weren't quite dead. Some of them stuck them into the girls.

My mother walked down to the woman's neck. Her breath was so shallow now, she was almost gone. She wasn't moving at all. I stopped in front of her eyes. I'd never seen such large eyes in my life, and the colors—I can't describe them. Like no colors on earth, and the colors moved and shifted like strands of jewels dancing in starry waters. I think she saw me. I'll never know. She gave a shudder, and one long sigh, and then I could tell she wasn't staring at me or anything else on the beach anymore.

Come on. My mother, standing in a river of blood, her machete and half her body red and wet. *You killed her,* I said.

She was dying anyway. She comes here to give birth on the beach and die, that's what her kind does.

And she gives birth to us? That's how we were born?

Mom nodded. *That's right. We don't give birth to girls. We're not allowed. And this thing,* she pointed to the body, *only gives birth to females. So, I got you here, and my mother got me here, when we came out of the ocean in someone like this, many years ago.*

But Dad said we'd be coming back with a boy, remember? That you were going to have a boy.

Mom pointed to one of the creatures. *That's what he does. That's what he's good for, every time. Next year, we're both giving birth, and we can keep them if they're boys.*

In the distance, the women let out a shout. They had split open the stomach with their machetes, and masses of blood and placenta were spilling across the beach. Inside the thick gore, round objects, no larger than beach balls, rolled and spun.

But Mommy. I was starting to cry. I didn't understand what she was saying, what she meant. I placed my broken hand against my stomach. *I'm pregnant? What happens if I'm pregnant with a girl? What happens to the girl babies if we're only allowed to have boys?*

And Mom let out this long sigh like I was just SO stupid, and gave me a funny, tight grin, and said, *What makes you think your brother and your dog are the only bodies buried in the backyard?* And she walked away from me toward the eggs, dragging her empty net.

I walked back up to the woman's outstretched hand, and stood there for the longest time, my five small fingertips against the massive whorls of her rough skin, thinking about all the smooth flat rocks I sat on and skipped across in our backyard, and all the times when I was really little and Mom wore those pretty loose-fitting dresses and how instead of hugging her, she would only let me hold her hand. And then the sun broke through the grey clouds, and it was really low in the sky, and everything just lit up so lovely and bright, all the black sand and the steaming red mounds of organs and the white hills of flesh everywhere and the woman's beautiful dimming eyes. Wide rivers of shit and afterbirth and viscera, blossoming into dark clouds as they slid under the waters. And those eggs being packed into the nets and dragged up to the empty cages, those gross pink sacs that we, that I, were stealing out of the dead giantess, that a bunch of strangers would be mothers to for the rest of their lives. Just like all the women on the beach. Just like me. And all the seawater and semen running down my purpling legs, and now the walls opened up and men in hazmat suits came out with giant axes and bone saws and ran toward the body, and wet shards of the dead giantess spurted into the bright morning sky and the seagulls went joyfully insane.

And I looked up at the sunlit wall, all those black-suited men and boys staring and talking about the other women and me, still making their little observations and notes, still with their cocks in their hands, laughing and staring down. And this was the beach I was born on, the beautiful beach of my childhood, and everywhere I looked, there was nothing but grime and foam and ugliness and death.

And that was the end of summer.

The Dunes, August 29th

Anyway. Yeah, so. Family reunion.

I don't know what happened to all the parts of the giantess's body. More men came, and carted everything away, and then they worked nonstop on dismantling the wall. It'll be shipped off to some other town that needs it next. We'll be driving back to Tacoma in a couple of days. And then school starts, which is just so weird to think about that I can't even. Funny, though, how all the boys I could never find all summer long or who were never interested have suddenly shown up, hanging around the cottages of me and the other girls, totally paying attention, totally competing for us, making sure we don't forget them when we're gone. Even the man who pretends to be my father looks at me strange when the woman who calls herself my mother isn't around, although I stare him down so hard he knows he'd never fucking dare. I don't know, now that everyone knows I'm pregnant, maybe they think I'll be a good wife, a good mom to what they hope will be their son. Yeah, everyone wants a good catch. Or maybe they're just pretending. Maybe they're keeping track of me like they were on the wall. Maybe they're afraid of what I'll do to them if their backs are turned, what I'll do to them like the wave of a hard ocean storm.

Someday.

AND LOVE SHALL HAVE NO DOMINION

craigslist > hell > district unknown > personals > missed connections > d4hf

Date Unknown

human star, are u my gate to the world?—(central park west, August 2003)

it was the night of the blackout—do u remember? time is as one to me time is nothing to me time is nothing, but in ur linear existence it was Then, it was the night the city closed her hundred million eyes. one hundred degrees and still rising as heat bled up from the buildings and streets, anxious to escape into the cool of space, never again to be bound. u were walking up the western edge of that man-made forest in the hard pitch of night, humans stumbling all around, flailing and quaking under an unfolding sky of stars they had never before seen, or simply forgotten existed. humans, brilliant with the Creator's life like star fire and u the brightest of all, but red and gold and white like my fallen Majesty, my sweet Prince, shining in the cesspools of earth he eternally spirals through, a necklace of diamonds crashing over shit-covered stone. and i? i was wandering to and fro upon and over the world, as our divine Prince taught us, and as i glanced down i caught the faint flash of a spark. that is what

157

drew me down and in, the force and fuse of life that comprises ur soul. u felt it 2. do not deny: i know u saw the thick branches of the trees bend and toss in my wake, rippling and bowing before my unseen passage. i saw ur eyes widen, and the bright gold fuse of stargodfire coil in ur heart, darken and drop lower. u quickened ur pace, but u never stopped staring into the primal green mass, ur desire rising with the heat with the wind with every thunderous vibration of my coming. mystery power and the unseen currents of un-nature, revealed in the absence of confusion of un-light and machines—these things drew ur most inner self toward me even as u turned away walking up the long walled side of the forest, running ur hand against the ancient rock, fingers catching thick moss and small weeds, soft fingers scrabbling over hard cold granite sparkling-veined with the crushed bones of things long past. and the wall became my body my horns my mind and i lapped at ur creamy thoughts and the city shuddered in unease, and so did u.

all parts of u all fissures all hollows all voids will i fill until u open ur mouth and there is only my voice / open ur eyes only my sight / touch ur cunt only my cock / slice ur flesh bleed only my tears.

no need to respond. u will. u already have.

Date Unknown
a thousand times ill-met, yet not met once—(fifteenth floor, office building, midtown, 2005)

u were at a work machine, shaking a malformed manmade thing—fine sprays of obsidian liquid shot up, landing against white silk and skin. the last of the ink, spent against lonely flesh. do u remember this day? laughter, floating across the floor. and u dropped the object, put ur hands to ur throat as u fled to ur women's rooms, where u sat on cold porcelain and cried, wondering what to make of such a life, a life so open to wonderful wide pain, and yet so mean, so small. u wept, and i licked at the tears—u felt me. fear leapt and coursed through ur body like a hunted hart. but u did not flinch or scream or draw away. i have trained u well—contact such as this in the public arena of slithering man has taught u to suffer my touch in silence, feigning ignorance. my talons slithered up ur thighs, leaving beaded trails of red against ur skin, and while u shuddered in silent terror and pain, i thought of many things.

i thought of u.

i have traveled now, many times through time, threading back through ur life to childhood, to the very first breath. with each stitch i stole, with each nip of the needle and thread of my will and desire, a moment of joy, of hope, of love, of beauty, of wonder was snipped from ur life like cancer, working open the hole through which i will inevitably enter. age two, sitting in ur front yard under the spring's warm sun, watching ur father plant flowers that later burst into glorious blooms—/—that later withered into putrid stinking masses at the touch of my vomit and piss. ur first true memory, forever changed, because i made it so. ur dog ate those decaying flowers, and died. u wept in ur little bed, and i sifted down through starry night and raised u high in ur nightmares toward them, showing u the whorls of the milky way as i nibbled the tears away. working working working, i stitched myself into every moment of ur life—even at the start, when my clawed hands twisted u from ur mother's womb in a gyre of blood—until the pressing horror of my unseen presence was as familiar and constant as the rain, the hole as wide as the reach of the magellanic. i am everywhere and everywhen: there is no moment when i have not existed for u / prepared for u / planned for u / toiled for u. and now, there is no moment in ur life when u have not existed for me. do u love my work, love?—but u love nothing now, nothing u can see, nothing u can taste or touch with the meaty cage by which u are bound. this is my work, and all those unbidden moments of heart-cracking loneliness, covering ur years until u can barely take a breath, until u long for anything except where and what u are? u are welcome.

despair of everything, my love, even ur pretty blouse, but never despair of this:

we shall soon meet.

Sat Oct 23

of all the things I've made—(apartment, west chelsea, 2009)

u are the finest. our terror / our pain / our horror / our screams / our blood that pours from ur skin as i rake it with horns/talons/ teeth. my flame-haired shooting star plummeting to earth and u know it is me u are falling into, and u cannot stop. i clear the path like a maelstrom—books and crockery dashed to ur floors, chairs swept aside, food rotted and flyblown with my single breath. un-lights explode, and in the darkness i expand like disease, driving friends / family / lovers / life from ur world. do u not understand? when we are as one, there will be no room for any of this in ur world. no room, no need. only our need. only mine.

u were sitting in that part of the building u have claimed as ur own, curled up in the corner of the largest room, on the larg-est cushions. images flickered in and out from a screen, and u watched them in silence as u drank yet again from the glass cup in ur steady hands. many times had the sun risen and set over ur city since i last touched and tasted u, laid waste to the possessions u think u love. the screen flickered. u swallowed ur wine and smiled. i watched the soft glint of hair at the back of ur neck, the fine lines around the corners of ur mouth, the curl of ur plump pink toes. untroubled breath, as even and smooth as the beat of ur heart. life, creamy placid and it washed over me, and and andand outside, afternoon sank and evening spread indigo feel-ers throughout the canyons of machines, and all over the world the swarming insect masses lit their candles and fires and devices, desperate pathetic futile in their attempts to hold night at bay, but firm in conviction. safety like their prayers, false and comforting. no different than u and i. and the little machines ticked the time away and the screen grew dark and u crept to bed. unlight washed in from the streets, dappling neon flashes from cars and signs, oranges yellows reds. and carefully, carefully: i hovered over ur sleeping flesh, sinking as slowly as the constant decay of space. ur heartbeat weakened, ur breath deepened—i tasted fear, felt the cold familiar terror envelop u. a dream i came to u as—a nightmare, and u frozen in my grip. but yes. yes. i descended, sliding my arms around u, the phantom lover of ur dreams, dark and dangerous, all-enveloping. and u unfroze, ur body pooling against mine. we lay together under the unfurling universe, my exhaling breath caught by ur inhalations. so soft and warm, so perfect a fit. as if this is what we were made to be.

do u remember Catala, on the beach, thirty-six years ago, before it sank into the sands? u were only twelve, and u fell through the rotting deck of the beached ship while looking for treasure. i stayed with u for a day and night, until they found u. i made the cold ocean waters warm and kept the crabs and gulls at bay, and i put my hand on ur heart and held u ever so tight, my horns and wings ur shelter, my body ur bed. i thought u saw me, through the veil of your tears. i thought u smiled. i thought i kissed ur lips. i may be wrong.

no, that memory is gone. it never happened. i ate it away; and then i broke ur legs.

human star, do u remember this night, this moment? remember it now, for tomorrow i shall wander to and fro again, back into the night into this pocket of time very pocket this NOW and i shall cut and fuck and burrow and rape my way into us and devour devour DEVOUR us until it has never happened until until we have never until until until FUCK FUCK FUCKING COCKSUCKING CUNTFUCK laksd WOEIFF

D; kd Ski;fkLKFKDsdjSkdL LKDF ll;SIE ldssd;

o

Sat Oct 23

iron fist in a pale-skinned human glove—(apartment, west chelsea, 2009)

star nursery of my desire, womb of my existence, do u remember this afternoon remember this afternoon and how it bled into the night like the child u had in windy ellensburg, the girl u left in long glistening strands of plasma redblack gouts of soft flesh blood on the floor of the bathroom as i stroked ur salt-wet hair, great rending sobs and the quaking pain splitting through ur curves ur tears lost like catala in the fires of my touch

no.

NO NO NO

do u remember this afternoon, pale and grey in ur endless grey city, open-mouthed ziggurats gnawing at the sunless sky? u stood at the window, wine glass full and dribbling in ur hand, staring at scudding clouds tentacling their way over silent-screamed rooftops, that familiar buzz undrowned by the drink, that familiar whisper and soft thundered deja-vu that this day was happening again. yes. ur breath fogged the window, and u placed the glass on the sill, raised ur hand to wipe it away, and—within that sliver of a second as the tiny beads of moisture floated off the glass u saw me behind it, saw the glint and gleam of my eyes, the curve of my fanged smile, the heft of my fist and all the attendant power and glory of the universe, all the secret places the Creator has forever kept from u all the stretches of dark matter and the knowledge that blossoms under the light of a hundred billion alien suns. u saw all, and the blood rushed into the core of ur flesh surrounding the stargodfire and u staggered back from the glass, pissing urself as I burst into the room, slamming through u like an errant asteroid. U hit ur head on a table, small moans seeping from grimacing lips but no time to scream or shout because this isn't happening how could this happen this only happens in dreams. I grabbed ur ankles and swung u around, my footfalls like lightning strikes against the polished stone, and ur fingers grabbed at tables chairs fallen books the edges of doors, and I rose u high like a flag, ur hands sliding up the doorframe, little threads of blood left behind with ur nails, and I ripped ur garments like tissue like breath like clouds and thrust my wriggling claws up inside, and finally u screamed, and in the bedroom against the quilts and childhood blankets I threw u down, pressing pressing and still u screamed in a city that only ever screams, only ever the sound of our breath the low dark explosions of my heart and clap of wings and the endless thrum of traffic and the uncaring world outside. I punched ur face and blood sprayed benedictine against our mouths, broke ur wrists down against the cloth, forced ur legs wide open my talons biting ur flesh ur cunt dark red and raw like a setting sun and I sunk into u my barbed cock splitting working working the hole and o god the bright gold fuse, the Creator's spark so close and my tongue deep in ur throat and my fingers against it choking and ur breasts soft warm scratched a thousand times by scales and I rammed u rammed u rammed u and this world so close now so close to everything that had ever been torn away

small fingers against the curve of my tail, u smiled

what have i

there, there, and ur sobs so soft and low and u spoke a word, a single gold fused plea passed from ur lips to mine i drank it in a gossamer silken wisp of the Creator, of u: and i slowed, i slowed. o my love, i slowed.

Sat Oct 23

is this what Humans want?—(bedroom, west chelsea, 2009)

this day i have plunged into a hundred thousand times, and all about us the universe spins and reverses, spins once more, once more. do u remember this day, this afternoon, this evening, unfolding again and again and again, unfolding like the bruised cream white of ur thighs, the swollen purple dusk of ur sex, the blood-split lips of ur quivering mouth? i sliced into ur beach like the catala, i thrust the sands apart, and there was no resolution, no joining, and the golden red stargodfuse flickered and floated in the unreachable distance as i lay spent between ur wet dunes, rusting, sinking into entropy and decay. that moment, that slow delicious moment, i have yet to find again. u said nothing u say nothing, every troy-like day upon day, u flinch and grimace and turn away and i pin ur face like a wriggling insect crushing ur jaws with my nails until the bones grind and bend, roaring and biting obscenities into ur tongue, and still u do not speak. do u remember it, that single slow moment when our eyes met, when u truly saw me, when u touched and whispered to me as a lover? i think i no longer do. i think it was a human infection, a trick of the Creator, a cancerous dream.

shadows sifted through the room like ghosts, cast from the same clouds, the same sun, the same sky as ten thousand days before. they are as familiar now to me as ur body against the red-stained sheets, staring past the ceiling into a future i cannot fathom or divine. my hand pressed down on ur chest, feeling ur heart gallop under all the layers of bone and skin, and u grew quiet and ur breath stilled and daylight crept from the room. i thought many times of peeling u apart, burrowing clawing through the layers into ur dying center, gnawing the bones and piercing ur eyes with the shards, snapping each rib one by one by one until ur lungs grew still and the arteries drained and ur small firm heart nestled against my palm, until i bathed in all the molecules of ur meaningless life, draped myself in ur soul, and rose anew, as one with everything u ever were.

how everything changes with a single word

how do u live ur life like this, so apart from everything in this vast existence except ur distant Creator, so at peace with being alone, apart. we lay next to each other in blood and piss and tears, my horns tangled in ur matted hair, our breath winds in and out of the others lungs, and ur eyes see nothing, ur skin feels nothing, u do NOTHING to seek me out, to discover what terrible invisible glorious power binds u to this moment, compels u to relive this day again and again. all my work, all throughout time, to make u pliable / soften resolve / sweeten despair / sharpen fear, so long have i toiled and crashed against uFUCKING LOOK AT ME LOOK AT ME SEE ME. see me like u did that first day that one time please i beg of u SPEAK TO ME O human star o love. are u a test. have i failed.

do u remember the word u spoke to me. do u remember the smile. will u not give these again? must i bite and scratch and claw it out of ur face and cracked teeth clattering down as i pull apart the cartilage grind the tongue meat forked and shredded searching seeking destroying but u do not remember. i eat each day and vomit it up and gorge it down again, until everything u ever were in me resides, the fuse that drives u mine.

must i take everything. do i.

yes

Date Unknown
a Gnossienne of the Heart—(unknown)

do u remember when i left u? do i remember when u left me? Time is measureless to me, Time is as air is as the dark wounds and tears through which i travel unseen and endless horizonless alone. and the city spreads out below me glittering sequins of tiny human souls thrown down against a net of electric fire an inferno of falsity and lies encased in canyons of profane steel. and i but rancid garbage caught in the dervishes of machine-made wind, adrift and without purpose. o my Prince, is this what u see, u feel, as u wander to and fro amongst ur souls? and the forest below is still, and ur brown-stained bed sheets empty.

Time is weight. Time is measured calculable movements of

human-forged horror, each as slow and meaningless as the one behind and before, Time a river, Time a great hooked chain dragging us to no place with no purpose, tethered bits of flesh. Time divides.

o empty star, each day i descended into the churning engines of Time, of un-nature and un-light, i descended amidst static and disruption, iron blades backwards, clocks unwinding, water in circles recoiling fast away. and the hospital shuddered at its granite foundation, patients vomited and bled, tongues spewed languages long dead, and all things foul and fair cried out as i worked worked worked against Time. before ur bed ur wasting flesh i stitched myself to the fetid air, commanding u to arise, to wake and fall into my arms, to say the Word as u had once said it before. walls cracked and mirrors shattered, and the Creator's minions scurried back and forth in their wine-dark robes, chanting His lies, evoking our brothers to save u. but my flies and shit kept all who thwarted me away, their eyes bled when they read His lies, and His book became as ash in their broken hands. again and again, i lowered myself upon u. u did not stir. milkglass eyes. parched lips. i placed my tight-sewn mouth ever so gently against urs, against ur nipples, ur cunt. everything u ever were is gone. everything i ever

no

in the indigo hour before dawn, in that fleeting sliver of light when i can catch my reflection in glass / silver / stone, i stare at the wide black gash of my mouth, now forever shut. cruel Prince, to give ur loved ones only half the knowledge, all the pain. beneath the thick iron stitches, swollen skin, bright gold stargodfire rests beneath my tongue, warm and alive. everything u ever were, everything u will ever be. everything i ever—

and the pain comes not blood or flesh or bone it rolls over me and the knowledge o sweet Prince the knowledge the burden of Time, the horrible skip of my heart. i have u have all of u possess u tight and neat and IT IS NOTHING. NOTHING. nothing.

and ur hand, so small, at the small of my back. what i would give. what i would give. and i cannot swallow cannot breathe. it is all that is left.

and in the indigo hour before dawn, after the quakes have subsided, i slipped between the rough sheets, curled by ur side. my hand so large against ur belly. ur hip warmed my cock, and my breath dampened ur breasts. and when i left, when morning chased me away, they found u bruised and beaten, ribs cracked, acid teardrops festering in the hollows of ur neck, skin dissolving like sand in the hissing waves.

o my human star. one second. one moment. one word. i have all of you and nothing, except one moment one word. i would give anything. i would give everything, to bring it back.

everything.

so.

Date Unknown

the last lost day—(ocean shores, washington, 1975)

and ur little body lay crumpled in pools of water, cold ocean-old pools of salt and sand and rust. the groan and crack of decaying metal all around, hiss of the waves rolling in with winds and night, and above u, the jagged hole still weeping with ur blood. beyond: endless darkening skies, and nothing at all. pain at one shoulder and fear at the other, clarion-calling each other like long-lost lovers, and the waters rising ever so higher, hitching up ur broken bones, ur flowered dress, ur slender shivering thighs. screams pure and high as starlight shot through the air, never breaching the hold, falling back down all around the cavernous waste.

u closed ur eyes. and the waves rushed and thumped against the wreck like the beating of some great unseen heart, and the waters lapped and caressed ur waist, slid across ur small breasts, lifting u up and down. and the cold grew in power and nimble fingers of water pushed the hair from ur forehead and eyes and black winged summer night closed in, around, down, furnace-warm but not enough to keep away the cold. and hard uncaring, unloving ocean covered ur lips, slid forked rivulets of brine into ur mouth, down ur throat and u breathed it in, and the world and the waves and the wind grew to pinpoint, ur body a million years away, and all that was left of the universe was nothing—/

/—was a kiss: a bright gold fuse of stargodfire unfurling from a single unstitched whispered word coiling into ur heart, an explosion of wings unfurling and lifting up, hot breath against ur face, warmth thunderclapping through ur blood and bones, and the roar of the waves thrusting against the beach, the hand at the small of ur back, a lover's touch at ur face as u opened ur eyes, standing alive and whole on the beach before the Catala, rusting high and dry above the grassy dunes.

and u stood shivering hound-like, dripping wet hand at heart, under the white gulls' cries, under the scudding clouds and the lowering sun, stood before the Catala, the ship with the hidden treasure, the ship u had never set foot on—/—fallen on bled on died. Stood until the nerves bit and prickled in ur legs, and the shadows lengthened and reached u, brushing against ur toes / the small of ur back / the tender hollow of ur neck / the translucent flesh of ur ear, all set afire by unseen whispers warning u away, and: u flew, a girl-shaped human star shooting up the long flat dunes through the grass and over the naked driftwood piles, racing away the miles of stone cold coast until u seemed as small and unreachable as the far-off circling gulls, never stopping, never looking back through all the joyful goldenfused years of ur life at the broken wreck back on the beach, the broken black-hulled monster rusting away, un-stitching un-working un-working, repairing all the broken moments until Time endless Time spiraling Time swept it all away, scrubbed it down to clean pure sand upon which my love, my memory, had no reach or purchase, until all that remained of the moment was U, and the

Glorious Word.
   do u remember now?
   u do not.
   i do.

THE UNATTAINABLE

...one thousand one...

There's a dream I once had long ago, a girlish fantasy I'd almost forgotten—and now I'm remembering it again, today of all the lonely days I've lived. I stand alone on the flat dirt of an arena. The flame-eyed stallion stares me down, foam-flecked lips curled back. He rears, slams his weight into the earth: I don't move. I know that by seeming not to see or care, I make myself the unattainable, the thing he longs for most in all the world.

And after time passes, the wild thing approaches, fear subsumed by curiosity. We dance in the empty center, limbs weaving rhythms hesitant, intricate, until I've mounted him. Now I'm astride his wide torso, hot muscles shuddering between my legs. He bucks beneath me, fights my weight against his heart. Yet I hold on, I will his fear to pass.

And it does, because he wants to be under my command, he wants to be broken. But it's only when I've ridden him pain-wracked to the ground, and still he pleads for my touch, do I know I've won. In the calm center of submission, when all that binds him to me are the reins of trust and love, I press against his steaming neck, and whisper in his ear:

"Now you're mine."

Of course, there are no feral things in this world. There are no flame-eyed stallions, no dragons to bestride. Nothing wild exists; and I'm old. Twenty years of bad jobs and nothing to show for it, except to turn tail and run across America, back to my old hometown. I'll fall into the void of my twilight years, and no one will remember me. At least, that's what I'm thinking as I drive the long curve of 97 into I-90. The hills part, and Ellensburg appears in the valley, backlit by the gold of the setting sun.

Twenty years haven't made a difference. College buildings still rise like neo-Gothic queens from the flat expanse, challenged only by the subtle mound of Craig's Hill and the white alien spine of the stadium. Cars stream ahead of me, ruby lights flowing into the town's throat. I roll down the window: hot air rushes over my face in dusty sheets. It's a wide and clean smell, like the scent of my first lover's skin, the night I lost my virginity on a sagging dorm room bed. He was a corn-fed stud, thick-limbed and heavy-cocked. I forgot how much I loved that smell, the taste of it in my mouth and lungs. I've forgotten so much, I realize.

Bright hoops of lights shine at the town's darkening edge, candy-colored tops gyrating above houses and trees. They disappear as I drop further into the valley, but now that I've seen them, I know what to listen for. Calliope music, high above the hum of traffic and wind, laced with the roar of a grandstand crowd. The sounds and lights mean the fair is in town, and with the fair comes the rodeo: horses and horn-crowned bulls, and all their men.

Tomorrow I'll cross the Cascades, drive to the house I was born in, slink inside. I'll sit by the window, remember all the things I lost in life because I was always dreaming of something else. This little town below me is the last bead on a necklace that's been falling apart for years—soon it'll slip off with the rest. All I'll have left is the wire that binds me to nothing, except useless childhood dreams.

That's when the old fantasy floods my mind, pushing reality aside. I shift in my seat, trying to shake off the weight of the late-August heat. Sweat trickles under my clothes, pools between my legs. I need a shower. Something wild, that's what I need. A pleasurable ache blossoms inside as I think of cool water, the rough hands of a stone-faced stranger running soapy hands over my breasts, while I lift one leg, guide the red tip of his flesh into—

A burst of horn snaps me out of the daydream. Wincing, I fall back, letting the car I almost rear-ended disappear in the traffic ahead. I rub my hands on my dress, clench the wheel and concentrate. And yet, my mind drifts. One thing I never did in Ellensburg, all those years ago. One last bead, one last sparking jewel. One last chance to catch it before it falls.

Hotel names float through my mind, but they'll probably all be full. It doesn't matter. I already know, wherever I end up, I'm going to stay the night.

…one thousand two…

Parking on the north campus lot takes half an hour, and the ride to the fairgrounds just as long. By the time I stumble down the shuttle steps, it's that odd hour before twilight, when a thin veneer of silver coats the shadows, sharpening the edges of everything. I pay the price and walk through the gate, stopping to look at the brick-red back of the grandstand. Crowds surge and disappear inside. The bulls will be in the arena tonight, the rankest beasts in the nation. Only eight seconds for each rider to hold on in order to place—but I know too well how eight short seconds can turn into a lifetime.

To my left, Memorial Park has been transformed into the midway, with Tilt-A-Whirls whipping screaming kids through the air. The stately O of the Ferris wheel hovers like a portal to another world. Odors of popcorn and sawdust, barbeque and leather saturate the air. It's like a big family picnic. I feel out of my element, clumsy—a middle-aged woman in a limp cotton dress, trying to get out of everyone's way. Wandering through the stalls, my eyes fix on men young and old. Men with children, men with wives and girlfriends, men with their buddies and friends. Stetsons and Levi's, clean-shaven faces and light-colored button-down shirts. All of them, with someone. A couple walks past, high school kids. The boy's hand is hooked into the girl's jeans, revealing smooth, tanned skin. Her hand rests on the back of his neck, playing with strands of hair. They're in love.

In a panic, I slip to the side of a cotton candy stand, away from everyone. What was I thinking? I don't belong here. This little fair isn't the Puyallup, where the midway blots out half the sky, where crowds of ten thousand clog the grounds. I could get lost there, unseen in the crush. But here, I stand out for what I am. A big-boned woman on the make. Floozy. Whore. Inside my dress pocket, the grandstand ticket crumples into a tight ball. Somehow it slips to the ground as I walk away.

A volunteer tells me where the exhibits are. She also points me to the beer garden—the look in her eyes tells me this is a woman who knows about the booze, because she'll be hitting it after the mid-way shuts down. I thank her and move on, determined to reach the stock barns before they close. Maybe I'll find someone there, some dirty stable hand who won't mind five minutes of humping in a cobwebbed corner with a desperate woman on the run from herself. It's a depressing thought, but it keeps me going.

I pause at the race track surrounding the stands. Behind the high chain-link fence, a horse approaches at bridle pace, the rider steering her down the dirt. A rush of noise from the grandstands, drowning out the announcer's metallic voice. Did someone get thrown, or did they win? I turn away, just as the cowboy catches my eye. Not that I wasn't looking. But it's the horse that makes me pause—a roan, glossy and tall, perfect form. She's a wonder, and when the boy hears my gasp of pleasure, he smiles.

Yeah, a boy. Barely out of his teens, so bright and flush with youth that it hurts to stare at his face. Yet when he winks, I blush and grin like a little girl. He's not my type, he's far too pretty and young, but I'll take what I can get, nowadays.

"She's beautiful," I say. The horse tosses her head, dark eyes looking me over from under a fringe of hair. *I don't submit,* her mouth implies, firm against the bit.

"Don't let her know that," the boy replies, as he steers her over to the fence. "She thinks too much of herself."

"May I?"

"Sure. She's gentle." The boy watches as I stroke the long muzzle, his eyes never leaving me.

"You do know you're headed in the wrong direction," he finally says. "Rodeo entrance is that way."

I point in the opposite direction. "Yes, well, the beer garden's that way." The boy laughs, and touches his hat.

"Well, ma'am, maybe I'll see you there later."

"I highly doubt it. You don't look old enough to drive."

"I'm driving her, aren't I?"

Now I laugh. "Oh, I think you have it backwards."

The boy winks. "Believe me, I'm old enough to do a number of things. I just might prove that to you later on." He guides the roan away, leaving me rolling my eyes even as I revel in the flattery. Turning away, flustered and unseeing by my small victory, I run smack into—

The words freeze on my tongue. The man standing before me stares me down with a face so sharp and cold, it's like being punched with black ice. By the time I've caught my breath, he's slipped into the crowd. People push past as I stand transfixed, shivering in the heat. All I remember of the face under the dark Stetson reminds me of Mt. Everest, in the black slits of his eyes, the weathered angles and peaks of his profile—a face I could die of exposure on. And why should I care to remember what he looks like, I don't want to think about him. Yet, I can't stop.

At some point I'm moving again, although I don't know what my destination is, or what will happen when I arrive.

…one thousand three…

I can't see the land around us, when his truck finally stops. But I know I'm near Kittitas, the small town just east of Ellensburg. I found him in the barn with the Black Angus bulls, and it took longer than eight seconds to get his attention. Yet somehow I convinced him, made him take pity on a woman with no home, no place to stay the night. So when the floodlights dimmed and the gate closed, he let me follow him out of Ellensburg and down quiet roads to his home—a small white bungalow surrounded by large trees and endless clear sky.

I cut the engine. As it ticks the heat away, silence blankets me, the kind found only between mountains, in the sleeping valleys and plains. It's like someone just took the pillow off my face, and let me breathe again.

He's already out of the truck, a large sheepdog groveling at his feet. A peaceful pleasure radiates from his face, erasing the sharpness of years. I watch him caress the dog's soft ears. Goosebumps and prickling nerves, like my skin is on fire, like my first date in high school—I never thought I'd feel that way again. I grab my bag and get out of the car. I'll make him forget about that dog, if only for this night.

Following him across the dirt drive, I walk up several steps to a sleeping porch. Face hard again, he opens the door, motions me inside. I slip past, feeling a bit like I'm trespassing. Honestly, I didn't think I'd get this far. He drove to his house so fast, I was chasing him most of the way.

"Have a seat." As I perch on a worn brown couch, he hangs his hat up, runs his hands through his hair. Without the wide felt curve framing his eyes, he loses a bit of the severity. He wipes his palms on his jeans, stares at the floor. One boot rubs at something invisible. Is he nervous?

"Beer?"

I nod, and he disappears into the kitchen. I sit for a minute, all polite and mannered, then decide he's giving me a chance to snoop. So I circle the room, gleaning for clues. What kind of man is he? Well, he's not stupid. The bookcase next to the TV set is full. I run my fingers along the spines: Pynchon and Kerouac sit next to McCarthy. Below them sits a shelf of thick technical manuals on agriculture. Several posters hang on faded cream walls—country landscapes, an Ansel Adams photo of the Rockies. No photos of him, though—nothing personal at all. I still know nothing about him, other than that he wants me here. I think, that is. If he wants to fuck, he hasn't shown much interest.

"You a reader?"

He stands in the doorway, beers in hand. There's a look on his face—amusement? Well, I can't pretend I wasn't snooping.

"Not much anymore. I got rid of most of my stuff when I had to move. The books were the first things to go."

He doesn't reply. Anxious to keep the conversation going, I slide one of the manuals out from the shelf.

"*Guidelines for World Crop and Livestock Production*. Light reading?"

"I'm not a light reader." He sets a beer onto the coffee table with a thump. The conversation on books is over, it seems. Frustrated, I sit back down on the couch. He returns to the edge of the door and takes a long pull from the bottle, his eyes never leaving me. I drink my beer, feeling self-conscious. It's like he's sizing me up, the way he'd size up a horse before deciding if it was worth the ride. It's a territorial stare.

Gathering up my courage, I stare back. His hair is longer than I thought, but there's also more grey in it than I noticed before. Dark brown eyes, and fine lines running from nose to mouth. My age, maybe older. Not beautiful, but compelling. His mouth *is* beautiful, I decide. Not the plump wet lips of a boy, but hard and dry, experienced—the mouth of a man. A sudden urge to feel that mouth moving over my breasts, between my legs, sends a violent shudder through me.

"Cold?"

"No," I mumble, playing with the label on the bottle as a blush warms up my cheeks. He saw me stare, knows why I shivered. Time to act coy. "I'll need sheets for the couch, though."

He shoots me The Look. I know that look. It's a sardonic half-smile, accompanied by raised eyebrows and the slightest of eye-rolls. It's the look my mother used to give me when I lied about not touching myself. I knew he wasn't going to make up the couch, that I wouldn't be spending the night there. We both knew it. And so he gives me The Look. It's like waving a red cape before a bull. I sit up, back stiff, face tense.

"What." It's not a question. It's a challenge.

He says nothing. Now it's a contest. But my impatience makes me crack. I keep my voice light, but I can't disguise the anger.

"What? What did I say that's so amusing?"

He shakes his head. "Please. You didn't follow me all the way out here just for my couch."

"Well, I didn't follow you out here because I'm a slut, if that's what you mean." I spit the words out like bullets. My mistake. His whole body shifts, like a snake's casual recoil before striking.

"Don't pull that shit on me." His low voice oozes polite menace. I ignore it.

"What shit is that? Enlighten me, please."

"Acting like you don't know why you came here. You're far too old to pretend you don't know what's going on." A slight twang has entered his tone, a bit of the country. I'd laugh if I wasn't so unnerved by him—yet I can't stop goading him. Fucking up my life overcomes my fear, every single time.

"Well. If I'm too old to understand you, then I guess I'm too old to fuck. Problem solved." I sit back and pound the rest of the beer.

"Put that down, bitch, and get over here. I don't have all night." He eyes his watch. "Some of us actually work, you know."

That's it.

"Fuck you!" I slam the bottle down and grab my bag. It's only five steps to the door, but I don't make it. All of a sudden he's just *there,* arms around me, same way he's probably done it a thousand times with animals wilder and stronger than me. As he spins me around, covers my face in hard kisses, I'm surprised by how good it feels to be grabbed, to be handled. There's no poetry in it, it's all need. I still want to hit him, but I was oh so right about those lips of his, and my whole body rocks with the overwhelming desire to fuck. He slams me against the door—I match the grind of his hips, panting as I spread my legs, rub my crotch against the hard bulge in his jeans. But when I reach for his zipper, he breaks away and drags me across the room, hand clamped firm on my arm. I stumble behind, lips and cheeks burning from his rough stubble, as if a ghost of him remains locked against my face.

The bedroom is dark, and he keeps it that way. The moon is bright, though, and I see everything: hard muscles, beads of sweat, the flame-red spark of his eyes….

…one thousand four…

There's no foreplay. He takes off his clothes with absolute economy of movement, while I let my dress fall to the floor, pushing it aside in a flowered crumple. I fall back on the bed, but I'm barely off my feet before he's crouched over me. Two thumbs hook into my panties, and they're ripped apart, gone. He's not looking at me, not touching me, not caressing me. I'm not here.

In the dim light, I see the ragged line of a scar across his lean stomach, glowing white against tan. It reminds me of that last sliver of light above the mountains, before the sun disappears. He spreads my legs wide, then places a hand against my shoulder, as if he thinks I'll bolt. He's not wrong. This isn't what I wanted, though—he's in complete control, there's no taming of anything happening here. Straining my neck, I catch a quick glimpse of his cock, long and hard as he strokes it, before he lowers and blocks my view. I close my eyes, grimace as he enters me. One expert stab, and I'm pinned to the sheets like a butterfly on wood. A gasp of pain escapes my mouth, but the hint doesn't take. He's fucking the hell out of me, and he won't slow down. But he doesn't make a sound—no grunts or groans, nothing to indicate pleasure.

The spackled ceiling overhead catches moonlight from the open window. I watch shadows dance in tiny patterns but they can't distract from the pain. I raise my arms, thinking if I put my hands against his chest, he'll slow. The movement triggers a violent reaction: he grabs my wrists and holds them against the mattress. I kick out, but he ignores me, probably doesn't even feel the blows. His cock pumps in and out, methodical and sure. Instinctive, against my will, my hips arc up in slight thrusts. My traitorous cunt contracts, grows slick. The pain doesn't lessen, but it doesn't grow worse. I'm not thinking of the ceiling anymore.

He presses down harder, crushing my breasts. Sweat trickles from his hot skin to mine, and I smell him, sharp and musky. A foreign scent, not unpleasant. He buries his head into my neck and hair. Hot breath floods over my skin as his mouth moves against me, murmuring some strange language I can't hear. Fear and anger dissipate, replaced with slow wonder. He's gone, somewhere so far away that I can't follow. Does he see me there? Am I in that dreamscape of his? He chose me. Even with that face, those dagger eyes, he could have had anyone. He wanted me. But, he's not with me.

"Stop," I say. He doesn't, and I try again. "Just stop for a second. Where are you?"

His sudden grab at my face is the last thing I expected. Two large hands hold my head tight. His lips brush mine as he speaks.

"What are you talking about?"

"Wherever you are, I'm not there. I'm right here."

He doesn't answer, only sighs before thrusting in again, like an engine that can't stop. I struggle against him, trying to keep him still, but he's too strong. He pushes down, pinning my arms between the both of us.

"You're hurting me," I say.

"Then make me stop. What are you afraid of? I can take it." The intensity of his words, the clotted growl of need and desire confuses me. Now I'm the one with no answer. Does he want me to punch his face, twist his balls until he does what I say? That's not my fantasy.

"Please, just slow down a little."

"Make me."

"What?"

"Make me." Pleading.

This is unsettling. "I can't *make* you. You're twice as strong as me."

"Goddamn, you're stubborn." Is he laughing at me now, or is it from despair?

"Fuck you. I'm not livestock. You can't break me."

"I've broken everything." Desolation and sorrow in his voice, so deep I don't think he even knows they're there.

"You can't break me," I repeat, voice cracking. Tears well in my eyes, but I refuse to cry. "You won't win."

A moment of silence. Then, out of the dark:

"I always win."

His mouth covers mine, tongue sliding inside. Protestation forms in my throat, but it dissolves. His cock demands my full attention, hammering away as if it had never been interrupted. God, it's so painful, and it feels so good. I can't help it—it's the way he moves his hips, the way the base of his cock and coarse hair rubs up against my clit, the slick pole of flesh filling me up. A perfect fit, like he was born for me. My nails dig into his back, barely able to keep a grip, mouth biting his shoulder as I come, thunderstruck into stiff spasms. A few more thrusts, and he stops—abrupt and matter-of-fact, like he lost interest. He rests on me, our hearts pounding in time together, with my muscles wrapped so tight around his cock, he couldn't leave me if he tried. All that, and he never uttered a single moan. He never came.

His head lies against my shoulder, breath light and untroubled. Do I dare? With the lightest touch, I caress his damp hair—a cautious attempt to show warmth. But the moment he feels it, he lifts up and pulls out of me, then rolls over, curling against the side of my body like a child.

He's asleep.

...one thousand five...

I stare at the ceiling. Beyond the roof of the house, stars run across the cloudless valley sky in silent flight. Everything sleeps below, dreamless and deep—horses and horn-crowned bulls, and all their men. Everyone safe at home, except for me. My hand creeps down to the matted hair, the throbbing folds of flesh. No one's ever fucked me as hard as he did, but I've never come like that before. I think of waking him, hoping he'll slide his arms around me, hold me tight—but the thought of his impersonal brutality keeps me still. And why didn't he come? Why did he fuck me with such violence, and for no apparent pleasure of his own, save that he could?

Well, that must have been the point: the bastard could. Leave it alone, I think. Let him sleep, before he wakes up and beats me to a pulp. I was lucky he didn't—I haven't been so lucky in the past. Rolling away from him, I slide the edges of the sheet over my worn flesh. I shut my eyes, concentrate on the wind in the trees, the passing of the stars.

But the hours drag, marked by electronic ticks of a digital clock on the bedstand beside me. I can't sleep, and now I have to pee. He hasn't moved, except to slip one foot over mine as he sinks further into dreams. If I get up, I'll wake him. But I really have to go, so I move, trying not to rock the bed as I pull my hair from under his head. He shifts, says nothing. I don't look back to see if he's awake, as I creep into the pitch-black bathroom. Only when the door's shut do I fumble for the light switch, and let out a sigh of relief.

The bathroom is sparsely decorated, much like the rest of the house. Under the glare of the light, I sit on the toilet and stare at the plain shower curtain, the half-curled tube of toothpaste on the counter, a chipped glass holding a single splayed-bristle toothbrush. Nothing on the walls except a mirror over the sink, and a small wreath of dried roses and crumbling greens. Not something a man like him would have bought in a million years. There was a woman here, once.

Flushing, I hobble to the sink and run the water till it's lukewarm. Wetting the corner of a bath towel, I pass it between my legs, ignoring the pain. It'll pass. In less than a day, I'll be home, and this will all be a distant memory, just another foolish, fucked-up dream—

I pull the towel away. The dull ache pulses like a second heartbeat. It's blood, rushing through all the secret places he once was. It's all I have of him, the pain of where he filled me up, where he left me. Do I want to erase it so quickly?

I empty the chipped glass and fill it with water. As I drink, my reflection catches my eye. The woman staring back is a strange but familiar one—the young girl of my past. A quicksilver ghost, fine-lined around the eyes and mouth, but all the more beautiful for aging. A pale face, surrounded by messy brown hair, red-tinged cheeks where his stubble burned the skin off, and a bright sheen drifting across dilated pupils. A drop of water hangs from my swollen lower lip. Is this what he sees? I imagine him standing behind me, hands cupping my breasts, mouth pressed against one shoulder in soft worship—an image so strong, I glance to my side to see if he's really there. I look back at the mirror.

What I could be, with him. If I want it to be.

"Stop it," I whisper. "It's just another dream."

But the image, the feeling, remains.

…one thousand six…

A knock at the door—the image dissolves. "I'll be just a minute," I start to say, but he's already opening the door.

"You all right?" He looks up and down my body, his face neutral.

"I'm fine. I was thirsty."

"Took long enough." He gestures, indicating that he wants in. I let him take the glass as I sidle past him, careful not to indicate my impulse to run.

"Don't fall asleep," he says before closing the door. I notice he keeps it open a crack. The thin line of light guides me across the mattress to the headboard, where I curl up and listen to the sounds of running water. Night pours in through the window like a river, in the rustling of leaves, the distant howl of a dog. The light flicks out, and I sigh. I don't want this again, all this rough handling, the impersonal stabbing of flesh. My heart pounds, unmoored and drifting—I curl up tighter, afraid it'll break through my ribs and float away.

He moves across the room, graceful and invisible. My body senses him standing over me, staring. I'm clutching myself like a child hiding in the closet from the monster outside, I'm trembling like a newborn colt. I want to shout *no,* my muscles ache, I'm battered and bruised. I want to cry, having him kiss the tears away. But he won't. He lowers.

The second time is like nothing I expected.

My hair slides back from my face—he's caressing it in careful strokes as he tucks it behind my ears. My eyes have adjusted, and I see all the sharp angles of his face softening. One finger traces my jaw line, moves up to my lips. His other hand rises—I brace myself, but don't turn away. His fingers suss out a length of hair, separating and smoothing it into three pieces. Something catches in my throat as I recognize what he's doing. He's braiding my hair, gently working the pieces into a single plait. His touch is comforting—inch by inch my legs unclasp, fall against his. Together we sit, heads bowed. Static crackles, and he licks his fingers before slicking the unruly strands down. My mother used to do that.

When he gets to the end, he ties it off—a hard and neat knot my fingers wonder at, while he turns my head and starts another braid. I shift closer, draping one leg over his. His knee rests against my cunt, soothing to the sore flesh. My left hand lowers onto his thigh, casual. He doesn't push me away. Inch by inch he works the plait, and I glide my palm up to the dark center, where he's all silky curves and tight curls. My fingertips find a home in the tangle of hair right at the base of his cock.

He ties the knot, then runs his hands over my face. Heat flares inside my cunt. His knee shifts, and I press against it, leaving his skin wet. He thrusts his hands into my hair, grabbing the braids, drawing me in. I don't have to see to know where his lips are—I draw his hot breath in on a sigh, let it seep back from my mouth to his.

"Don't go," he whispers. "Don't go." Each word is a kiss, a sigh, a plea.

"I'm not going anywhere." Inside, my heart sinks. Is he going to start this all up again? But his response surprises me.

"Don't go home." More kisses, and his hands drop to my waist, running over the wide curves. "Stay here."

"I can't stay, I have to get home—" The sentence trails off, disappearing in the other conversation between our lips.

"Your home's not there." His words are cruel, and true. Firm palms slide up to my breasts, where his fingers and thumbs begin rolling my nipples into stiff points. "You're running to nothing."

I have no answer, for him or myself. Just let him have his say. It's worth it. My hand travels up his hardening cock, to the plump tip. I rub at the small hole, working silky liquid out over the soft skin. He gasps, but shifts away, his cock sliding out of reach. Lips move to my nipples, then lower. As I fall back onto the pillows, his wet mouth courting my cunt into delicious submission, it finally sinks in: this is a competition. An event. He's going to make me come like the animal I am, then walk away before I can give him one second of pleasure: because he's the one in control. And I'll be left naked in the dust, pleasure and pain ringing my bones like bells.

I've broken everything. I always win. Isn't that what he said?

He wraps himself around me, sinks into me, and once again I drown. He doesn't come, and he won't tell me why. Hot tears and pain follow the orgasm; but this time he holds me, rocking me like a child as the night bleeds into pink dawn. Exhausted, liquid-limbed, I sink into delicious half-sleep, floating through fragments of dreams. The land lies all around me: I am the Cascades, ice-capped peaks covered by his star-shot skies. And somewhere in between, three words thread their way through us, a radio whisper of the heart drifting from one slumbering body to the other. *Let me submit.* I reach the black lands of sleep, a frisson of fear pushing its way in with me, as I realize I don't know where the words came from—from me or him, from the mountains or the sky.

…one thousand seven…

Sunlight and bird song. Before I stretch out, open my eyes, I can tell he's already gone. The wake of his leaving fills the whole house with bittersweet calm.

A thin plaid robe lays on the edge of the bed. It wasn't there last night. Folds pressed into the fabric tell me it hasn't been worn in years. I slip it on, and raise a sleeve to my nose. His faint scent clings to the fabric. I smell him on my skin as well, and in my hair. My tongue glides over my lips. He's there, too.

I pad through the living room, reverent this time, as if I'm in church. The windows are shut, and dust motes hang in the air like dead stars. From the kitchen, a clock ticks out the seconds. I follow the sound. Midday sun drenches the room, bleaching the curtains white. I smell strong coffee and the sulphur whiff of eggs. A mug sits next to the pot—I pour a cup and lower myself into a chair, still a bit stiff from last night. I don't feel bad, though. I haven't felt this calm, this balanced, in years.

He left a note and a map on the table, under a wax-red apple. I slide the note toward me, and read. Neat cursive letters in blue pen rest on the lines:

> *Working the fair today. There's a plate for you in the oven. Take what you need from the fridge.*
>
> *I'll be home around eight.*

A plate in the oven—I swing around, catch the handle and open the oven door. Warm air hits my face. A plate covered in aluminum foil sits on the rack. I grab a dish towel and pull it out, peel the foil away. Bacon, eggs and toast. He made me breakfast.

I pour another cup of coffee, and start to eat, staring at the note all the while. No "thanks for everything", no "it was great". Well, it's not his way. I unfold the map. He's drawn a dotted red line from the middle of nowhere, through Kittitas up to I-90. A note, an apple, and the way out. After all his protestations, he wants me gone. He wants me—

"Home," I say to the ticking clock. But the word doesn't sound right anymore. Maybe because, when I think of home, I don't know what it is I'm supposed to see.

My dad once told me that no man could live in an oasis. He could stop and drink, rest a bit, but then he had to move on, find his way home. This is only an oasis, I say as I wash the dishes and place them in the plastic rack. It was a place to lay in the shade, away from the burning sun. I stand in the shower, curtain open, staring at the wreath on the wall. It was only a place to get a little rest, before pushing on. The braids grow fat with water, and I don't undo them. My eyes blur—from the soap. I smooth down the sheets and plump the pillows, pressing each soft feather mound to my face before laying it on the bed. He'll sleep on them tonight.

I have to go.

I could have snooped through all his things, but I don't. He deserves better from me. But on the way out, I peek into the second bedroom, unable to resist. A flick of the light switch reveals boxes and cartons, an old steamer trunk, musty sheets covering tables and chairs. I lift a sheet, revealing a short bookcase.

Here he is.

Trophies, plaques and ribbons, all proclaiming the same thing, for the same event. *FIRST PLACE. FIRST PLACE. FIRST PLACE.* The dates—he won some of these in Ellensburg, the same years I lived here. We fought and bled and slept in the same little town, under the same starry skies. I let the sheet drop.

An open box sits high in a pile—I pull it down, and flip through a series of photos in cheap frames. A young man, jet-black hair framing a stern and determined face, riding bull after massive bull. Behind him sits a sea of faces: judges and grandstand crowds, with floodlights shining down on man and beast. Odd to see so much power and rage, muted behind framed glass. In one photo, the bull's kicked back so high, his hind legs are higher than the rider's head. But none of the photos show the rider falling. He's marking out his eight seconds, every goddamn time. The rage in the photos is the rider's, not the bull's. This is a man who always wins, who never lets go of the reins.

And yet he let go of me.

I pack the photos into the box, and balance it back on the pile. I'm careful to close the door behind me, just like it was before. My watch says two o'clock, I have to be on the road. A good six hours of driving are ahead of me, and I want to cross the pass before dark. The lights are off, the windows shut, and everything's tidy in the kitchen. I take the note and the map, leave the apple behind. I struggle to lock the front door, then realize it doesn't, and probably never did. There's no need for it out here. Amazing.

Throw the bag on the seat, rev the engine, and don't look back. It feels good to be on the road again, to be free. So it didn't turn out quite like I planned—when did anything? Buildings whoosh past in a blur as I speed through Kittitas, up to I-90. It was an adventure, something I'll remember when I'm old, when there's nothing else left to remember. One last bead from the string, flame-bright like the eyes of some rough stranger, caught in the palm of my...

...

...I'm standing by my car. It's parked on the lookout, a half-oval of dirt next to the highway, high above the valley. From here I see Ellensburg, see the glimmer of the Ferris wheel, the sparkle of windows and headlights caught in late afternoon sun. Kittitas lies to the east, green jewel in a strand of ancient land left scrubbed by the Cordilleran floods of ten thousand years ago. To the left sits Cle Elum, another small tree-dappled town. And in between, rivers of roads, a patchwork of farms and ranches. The land teems with life from the horizon's edge up to the snowy Cascades.

This is no oasis. This is an empire.

I'll be home around eight, the note in my hand says. I've been staring at it for three hours now, almost four. My skin burns from the sun. *I'll be home.* He's a careful man, economical with words. That much I know to be true. Three things he wrote that I needed to know, and left the map for leaving. What purpose, then, in telling me when he'll be home? Why should I care if he's home around eight? That's when I'm supposed to be back—. I won't make it now. He's won again. Has he ever lost?

Night's closing in. The sun's still high, but the light's changed. I look beyond the mountains and see nothing, feel nothing. The only thing I feel is in my hands—on a slip of paper, in a single cryptic sentence. Turning around, I reach through the open window and pick up the map. A dotted red line with two round ends. The circles look like the eyes of a bull, burning through paper streets. An animal who's always won, who's never been allowed to surrender. What would his fantasy of love be, then? What would be the unattainable for him?

Let me submit.

Traffic's a bitch. The fair's closing, and horse trailers and RV's clog the streets. I inch my way through Ellensburg to Kittitas Highway, then gun the motor till I'm back at the house, tires spraying gravel across the scraggly lawn. The windows glow pumpkin orange from the setting sun. Early evening winds whip the braids across my face as I unlock the trunk, root through boxes. At the bottom: thin leather straps and bronze workings, attached to six erect inches of polished wood. I could be wrong. What if he hits me—or worse? The note is damp with sweat. I clutch it, pray I'm right as I stumble up the steps into the house.

Everything's as I left it. I open the windows, turn on a light. He'll see my car, I can't hide. I don't want to. Let him know the rider has mounted, the event's already begun. I leave the bedroom dark. By the light of the setting sun, I slip off my clothes, strap the harness around my hips, and climb onto the middle of the bed.

The clock ticks, the wind sighs. Shadows stretch across the room. I wait, patient—the apple at my feet. The clock hands near eight. An engine, faint in the distance, growing nearer, until it throbs through the open window, then cuts. I don't breathe.

Footfalls against the earth, running. The slam of the door, the pound of boots like hooves against wood. He's rushing down the hallway, down the chute—

…one thousand eight…

There's a dream I had long ago, a girlish fantasy I'd almost forgotten—and now I remember it again, tonight of all the lonely nights I've lived. I wait alone on the flat white plain of the arena. My flame-eyed stallion stares me down, lips curled back in rage or shock: I am unmoved. Arms outstretched, erect, I look away. I know that by seeming not to see or care, I make myself the unattainable, the thing he longs for most in all the world.

And after time passes, the wild thing approaches, shy fear

subsumed by curiosity, kissing my hands, my feet. I wipe the sweat from his skin, run my fingers over his body, passion flowing where once only loneliness lived. We dance in the empty center, bodies weaving rhythms hesitant, intricate—until, slowly, gently, I've mounted him. Now I'm astride the lean torso, hot muscles shuddering under my legs. He bucks beneath me, fights the pain, fights my weight against his heart. Yet I hold on, I will his fear to pass.

And pass it does, in the shower of pearl-studded pain: because he wants to be under my command, he wants to be broken. But it's only when I've ridden him pain-wracked to the ground, and still he pleads for the pleasure of my touch, do I know I've won. In the calm center of submission, when all that binds him to me are the reins of trust and love, I press against his tear-streaked neck, and whisper in his ear:

"Now you're mine."

PUBLICATION HISTORY

"Panopticon" was first published in *The Magazine of Bizarro Fiction* #4, November 2010

"Stabilimentum" was first published in *Shadow's Edge*, ed. by Simon Strantzas, Gray Friar Press, 2013

"Wasp & Snake" was first published in *The Lion and The Aardvark: Aesop's Modern Fables*, Stone Skin Press, 2012

"Cinereous" was first published in *Zombies: Shambling Through the Ages*, ed. by Steve Berman, Prime Books, 2013

"Yours Is the Right to Begin" was first published in *Suffered From the Night: Queering Stoker's Dracula*, ed. by Steve Berman, Lethe Press, 2013

"Lord of the Hunt" was first published in *Aklonomicon*, Aklo Press, 2012

"In the Court of King Cupressaceae, 1982" is original to this collection

"It Feels Better Biting Down" was first published in *Nightmare Magazine: Women Destroy Horror*, guest edited by Ellen Datlow, 2014

"Allochthon" was first published in *Letters to Lovecraft*, ed. by Jesse Bullington, Stone Skin Press, 2014

"Furnace" was first published in *The Grimscribe's Puppets*, ed. by Joseph S. Pulver, Sr., Miskatonic River Press, 2013

"The Mysteries" was first published in *Nightmare Carnival*, ed. by Ellen Datlow, Dark Horse, 2014

"The Last, Clean, Bright Summer" was first published in *Primeval – A Journal of the Uncanny*, #2, ed. by Geoff Hyatt, 2014

"and Love shall have no Dominion" was first published in *Demons: Encounters with the Devil and His Minions, Fallen Angels, and the Possessed*, Black Dog & Leventhal, 2011

"The Unattainable" was first published in *Cowboy Lover: Erotic Stories of the Wild West*, ed. by Cecila Tan, 2007

ACKNOWLEDGMENTS

Thanks to the many writers and editors who have published and championed my work over the years: Robert Levy, Brian Keene, Ellen Datlow, Steve Berman, Laird Barron, Jesse Bullington, Cecila Tan, John Skipp, Robin D. Law, Nate Pederson, Robert Shearman, Simon Strantzas, Joseph S. Pulver, John Joseph Adams, Geoff Hyatt, Mike Davis, John Langan, Michael Matheson; and Paul Tremblay, who turns into a pickle if you say his name three times in a mirror. And now you know his terrible secret—you're welcome! Thanks also to my Patreon supporters for giving me a forum for creating some rather spectacularly filthy fiction. Apologies to my parents, Paul and Mary Llewellyn, who will once again have to pretend to the neighbors that they aren't mortified by my career choice—sorry! And special thanks to Ross E. Lockhart and Word Horde; and to Elinor Phantom, who I'm sure had something to do with the publication of this collection—cute dogs always seem to be in charge.

TITLES AVAILABLE FROM WORD HORDE

Tales of Jack the Ripper
an anthology edited by Ross E. Lockhart

We Leave Together
a Dogsland novel by J. M. McDermott

*The Children of Old Leech: A Tribute to the
Carnivorous Cosmos of Laird Barron*
an anthology edited by Ross E. Lockhart and Justin Steele

Vermilion
a novel by Molly Tanzer

Giallo Fantastique
an anthology edited by Ross E. Lockhart

Mr. Suicide
a novel by Nicole Cushing

Cthulhu Fhtagn!
an anthology edited by Ross E. Lockhart

Painted Monsters
a collection by Orrin Grey

Furnace
a collection by Livia Llewellyn

The Lure of Devouring Light (April 2016)
a collection by Michael Griffin

Ask for Word Horde books by name at your favorite bookseller.
Or order online at www.WordHorde.com

"A lavish, sumptuous tapestry of luxurious surrealism and strangeness."

—*The Horror Fiction Review*

TALES OF CRIME & TERROR EDITED BY ROSS E. LOCKHART

GIALLO FANTASTIQUE

CESARE   KAZEPIS

COOK   KEENE

DRAKE   LANGAN

GREY   MARTIN

GUERLAIN   PIERCE

JOHNSON   TOBLER

AN ANTHOLOGY OF ORIGINAL STRANGE STORIES at the intersection of crime, terror, and supernatural fiction. Inspired by and drawing from the highly stylized cinematic thrillers of Argento, Bava, and Fulci; American noir and crime fiction; and the grim fantasies of Edgar Allan Poe, Guy de Maupassant, and Jean Ray, *Giallo Fantastique* seeks to unnerve readers through virtuoso storytelling and startlingly colorful imagery.

What's your favorite shade of yellow?

Trade Paperback, 240 pp, $15.99

ISBN-13: 978-1-939905-06-2

http://www.wordhorde.com

Like everyone else in the world, you've wanted to do
things people say you shouldn't do…

HOW MANY TIMES IN YOUR LIFE HAVE YOU WANTED
to slap someone? Really, literally strike them? You can't even begin
to count the times. Hundreds. Thousands. You're not exaggerating.
Maybe the impulse flashed through your brain for only a moment,
like lightning, when someone tried to skip ahead of you in line at
the cafeteria. Hell, at more than one point in your life you've wanted
to kill someone; really, literally kill someone. That's not just an
expression. Not hyperbole. Then it was gone and replaced by the
civilized thought: You can't do that. Not out in public.

But you've had the thought…

Format: Trade Paperback, 224 pp, $14.99
ISBN-13: 978-1-939905-11-6
http://www.wordhorde.com

ABOUT THE AUTHOR

Livia Llewellyn is a writer of horror, dark fantasy and erotica, whose fiction has appeared in numerous magazines and anthologies. Her first collection, *Engines of Desire: Tales of Love & Other Horrors*, was published in 2011 by Lethe Press, and received two Shirley Jackson Award nominations, for Best Collection, and Best Novelette (for "Omphalos"). Her story "Furnace" received a 2013 SJA nomination for Best Short Fiction. You can find her online at liviallewellyn.com.